"Please go, Jaz," Chantal said.

"No, ma'am. Not when you look at me like that. Not tonight."

"Please—"

"I'm staying." He began pulling the pins out of her hair, letting the flaxen waves fall where they might.

"Jaz—"

He ran his hands through the silken tresses, then undid the top buttons on her jumpsuit. "Chantal, I need your loving tonight. I need you like I never needed anyone." He knew she felt desire, but he wanted more. He wanted her to need him as much as he did her, wanted no uncertainty. He needed her to say yes in all the ways a woman could.

Her voice was a whisper when she spoke. "Sounds like lust to me."

"Sounds like lust," he agreed huskily, knowing he was walking a tightrope. "But it _hurts_ like love . . ."

Bantam Books by Glenna McReynolds

SCOUT'S HONOR
  (*Loveswept #198*)

WHAT ARE *LOVESWEPT* ROMANCES?

They are stories of true romance and touching emotion. We believe those two very important ingredients are constants in our highly sensual and very believable stories in the *LOVESWEPT* line. Our goal is to give you, the reader, stories of consistently high quality that may sometimes make you laugh, sometimes make you cry, but are always fresh and creative and contain many delightful surprises within their pages.

Most romance fans read an enormous number of books. Those they truly love, they keep. Others may be traded with friends and soon forgotten. We hope that each *LOVESWEPT* romance will be a treasure—a "keeper." We will always try to publish

LOVE STORIES YOU'LL NEVER FORGET
BY AUTHORS YOU'LL ALWAYS REMEMBER

The Editors

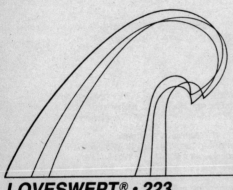

LOVESWEPT® • 223

Glenna McReynolds
Thieves in the Night

 BANTAM BOOKS
TORONTO • NEW YORK • LONDON • SYDNEY • AUCKLAND

THIEVES IN THE NIGHT
A Bantam Book / December 1987

LOVESWEPT® and the wave device are registered
trademarks of Bantam Books, Inc. Registered in U.S. Patent
and Trademark Office and elsewhere.

If you would be interested in receiving protective vinyl
covers for your Loveswept books, please write to this address
for information:

Loveswept
Bantam Books
P.O. Box 985
Hicksville, NY 11802

ISBN 0-553-21845-X

Published simultaneously in the United States and Canada

Bantam Books are published by Bantam Books, Inc. Its trademark, consisting of the words "Bantam Books" and the por-
trayal of a rooster, is Registered in U.S. Patent and Trademark
Office and in other countries. Marca Registrada. Bantam
Books, Inc., 666 Fifth Avenue, New York, New York 10103.

For Sandy & Lance
with love

One

Her skis glided through the heavy snow, fast and
smooth, as she swooshed her way to the crest of
the hill. Chantal Cochard stopped on the rise and
listened through the silence, every sense in tune
with the gathering storm rolling in over the mountains and the darting flight of chickadees looking
for shelter. Fresh flakes drifted down from the
broken sky, melting on her exercise-pinkened
cheeks and disappearing against her pure-white
one-piece snowsuit. Her cross-country skis were
white. Her boots were white. The hood covering
her mane of long blond hair was white. She was
invisible against the mountain.

Chantal glanced behind her, to the west and
the fading gray sun hanging low in the cradle of
the Rocky Mountains. The wilderness stretched
around her for miles, valley after valley of frozen
solitude. With a quick movement she pushed back
her right-hand mitten and checked her watch.
Four o'clock, and so far so good.

Kicking off again, she made a telemark down
the hill, the movements swift and sure as she
bent first one knee and then the other. Her skis

slashed a zigzag across the pristine slope. The forest came up to meet her, and within minutes she was deep in the trees. Lengthening shadows laced their way along the snow beneath the ponderosa pines and naked aspen trees, and Chantal slowed her pace. She stopped every few minutes to memorize the view behind her, looking for landmarks and tucking them in the back of her mind. A lichen-covered boulder silhouetted on a rise, the scythelike curve of a bent pine against the sky. This was her escape route, and she would be traveling it in darkness—after her job was finished.

A troubled frown reflected the intensity of her concentration, lending a firm set to the delicate features of her face, darkening the crystalline blue of her eyes. This was the last time she'd play this game, she told herself. She had said the same thing ten years before, but this time she meant it. She would get in, heist the necklace, and be curled up in front of her own fireplace in time to watch the sun rise over the Rockies. This one's for you, Poppa, and for Paul, she thought, and then it's over.

Another mile through the forest and then the multi-peaked roof of the Sandhurst mansion flickered into view through the pines. The gray shake shingles blended with the thickening clouds, smudging the lines between roof and sky. Negotiations for the million-dollar property had hinged on those shingles, Chantal mused. Using every ounce of her diplomacy, she had convinced the previous owner to replace part of the roof rather than lose his only qualified buyer in a year. Tonight she was going to scale those empyreal heights to repay a debt long overdue. There was no other way.

She moved in close enough to have a clear line

of sight of the long gravel drive and noted with satisfaction the bevy of Porsches, Mercedeses, and four-wheel drives clustered along it. Intermittent notes of music caught the soft night breeze and drifted toward her side of the mountain. The après-ski party was in full swing; the outside security system would be turned off—at least on the ground floor.

Chantal released her mountaineering bindings and settled in under a shelter of pine boughs. The storm front tumbled in over Independence Pass, dropping its frozen moisture in waves of heavy silence. And she waited, every move she'd make in the next four hours clicking through her mind. The storm passed, and by the time night had truly fallen, a full moon had risen to fill the landscape with shadows.

She slipped off her white pack and pulled a smaller, black one out. Adrenaline pulsed through her, warming her body and honing her senses. Her heart pounded and her throat got dry, and not for the first time she was tempted to turn around, to let the family's honor, or dishonor, die without her intervention. For the past ten years she had lived an exemplary life, subduing every rebellious urge, not daring to risk ruining everything again. But tonight she had to go against those years of careful training. There was more than honor at stake here, and what others had stolen from her family she was determined to return—one necklace of a hundred diamonds and a single perfect emerald.

She fingered the zipper of her pack, telling herself again and again that this was the only way. There would be no turning back. Tonight a debt would be paid in full and her life would be her own.

In minutes she was dressed completely in black, the turtleneck and form-fitting wool pants she had worn underneath her white down suit hiding her in the night. The white fur-lined hood was replaced with a black knit hat, and she carefully checked to make sure all her hair was covered. For her last piece of camouflage she exchanged her white boots for a pair of soft black leather sneakers. Then she pulled off her mittens and smeared blackface over her cheeks. She dabbed some on her chin and made one quick swipe across her forehead.

Her thin black gloves were looped over her belt, and she murmured a silent prayer as she slipped them on. Then, with only a quick glance to make sure her skis were well hidden, she slung the smaller pack onto her back and loped through the trees toward the south side of the house.

Jaz Peterson wedged his foot between two hunks of the natural stone wall of the north side of the Sandhurst mansion and heaved himself over the edge of the roof. All in all it had been an easy, free climb, even with eight pounds of rappelling gear bandoliered across his chest. The tricky part was going to be hanging in front of the eastern window of the library and cutting an opening in it. In truth, his biggest worry was getting caught in the act. If he pulled off the heist he was safe; he knew Sandhurst would never report the crime. Stealing classified documents to sell to the global opposition wasn't something Sandhurst—or anyone else in his position—would call the police about, no matter how ticked off he was.

When the Air Force had finally realized they couldn't put Sandhurst away yet, they had decided to do the next best thing—stop him. That was where Jaz came in. A call here, a flight there, and one Jasper Peterson, retired Air Force Intelligence, now a private investigator, found himself inching along a frozen roof in the mountains around Aspen, Colorado, instead of soaking up the sun in Mexico. There was no justice.

One little screw-up and you owed your life to those military types, he thought. Easy for them to ruin his life instead of sacrificing one of their own. Either way, this should square him with General Moore. And not for the first time Jaz wondered if a dishonorable discharge would have been so hard to live with. Certainly none of his clients gave a damn about his military record.

What clients? he thought with a snort. Thank heavens the fishing was free and the weather was warm in Mexico. He hoped the general reimbursed him for his time, or it was going to be another lean season lying on the beach in Cozumel. Maybe, and it was a hesitant maybe, it was time to abandon the expatriate game and come home.

Then again, maybe not. The general had mentioned payment in a roundabout way. What had he said? Something like, "I'll make it worth your while, Jasper."

In retrospect, that didn't sound all that promising. He and the general definitely had different ideas on what made things worthwhile.

Jaz anchored the climbing rope to a strategically placed chimney that was right where his information had told him it would be. But before he hooked his harness on, he stretched flat out on his stomach and edged his body partway over the roof, using his strength and an innate sense of balance to keep from falling off. The library window was dark. It was also a sheer expanse of plate glass from floor to ceiling, the whole house hanging over a seventy-foot drop into darkness. Jaz swore under his breath and eased himself back onto the roof. He'd expected the cliff, but the window was all wrong. Dangerously wrong. What in the hell was he supposed to do with one huge window? Whatever the general offered, he was asking for double. No, he was insisting.

Chantal worked herself up to the roof, her short stature making the overhang the biggest obstacle she had to overcome besides a serious dose of misgivings. Taking a deep breath, she curled her fingers around the drainpipe and swung her legs out from the wall and over the edge. The instant her foot landed, she pressed it against a shingle and pulled the rest of her body onto the roof. In the span of a heartbeat, like a cat, she was on the balls of her feet. With instinctive surefootedness and keeping a low profile, she pattered over the peaks and valleys of the roof, knowing exactly where she wanted to go.

When she reached the edge, she peered over it, found her balcony, then sat back to organize her tools. Out of her pack she pulled two thin magnetic plates connected with a wire, and a lockpick, which she stuck in her mouth. Crouching on the roof, she eyed the distance to the balcony one more time before lofting herself over the edge. She landed on her feet in a soft drift of snow, her hands already lining up the two plates.

She had gone over this scene mentally a thousand times, and from here on out every move counted, and every move had a time limit. Her mind was tight with tension as the seconds ticked away, but her body was loose, limber, her hands graceful and quick. She slipped the plates into the tiny gap between the French doors and slid them up until she felt the magnets catch on the contact points of the alarm system. Then she picked the lock. Forty-five seconds down and one question had been answered—she hadn't lost her touch. She didn't know whether to be pleased or dismayed.

As she swung the doors open, the wire connecting the plates kept the current flowing between the points so the alarm wouldn't go off. She didn't waste a thought on whether the soldering would hold. She had made the piece of equipment herself, and it was the best.

Knocking the snow off her shoes first, she slipped through the door, a shadow entering shadow. Her sneakers sank into the thick beige rug carpeting the gallery, silencing her steps as she sneaked through the arch to the library. She stopped and slid her lockpick back in its case, cocking her head and holding her breath to listen for silence. Party noise rumbled softly through the floor, but the library was hushed and quiet, with only her own heartbeat filling the void.

The draperies were open on the large window spanning six feet of the library wall. The full moon reflected off the scattered clouds and each crystal flake of snow, filling the room with vague light. Floor-to-ceiling bookcases swept around two other walls, all natural-colored oak and filled to the brim with volume after volume of knowledge. Chantal doubted if a single book had been opened, and on a whim she pulled out the closest one. The binding cracked as she opened it. She held it to her face; it even smelled new. She quickly tried two more at random, with the same results.

So much for the Sandhurst love of books, she thought, returning the leather-bound volume to its shelf. Jimmy Sandhurst's biggest thrill must have been dropping a few grand at the bookstore, and Angela probably had gotten a kick out of color-coordinating the whole shebang.

With her eyes now completely adjusted to the low light, Chantal scanned the room and found what she was looking for, the portrait of Angela Sandhurst wearing the emerald-and-diamond necklace. How appropriate, she thought as she looked up at the picture, how daring. It took a lot of moxie to have your portrait painted wearing stolen jewelry, but then, Angela wasn't known for her brains. On the contrary, Jimmy's trademarks were the deviousness of his mind and the stickiness of his fingers. Their real-estate negotiations had been a battle of wits. Chantal had barely gotten out with her commission intact.

A flash of irritation wrinkled her brow. She had responsibilities now. People counted on her, or rather, her money. The orphanage didn't know where the money came from, but Chantal knew that over the years her contributions had become part of their basic budget. Sandhurst had tried to take that away.

The thought eased her conscience another notch. Unlike that other night, this night would not leave a black mark on her heart. Good thing, too, she thought, because she didn't have any room left for black marks. Ten years of the straight life and innumerable contributions to charity had barely begun to ease her guilt over her heritage.

She stared up at the portrait, remembering the cut and impeccable quality of every stone. An arc of one-point diamonds curved down the side of the four-carat emerald. The intricately woven gold chain was punctuated by two lacy inserts of smaller gemstones. Angela wasn't wearing the earrings. The fence must have broken the set.

With a resigned smile curving one side of her mouth, Chantal acknowledged the red indicator light on the photoelectric transmitter above the picture frame. Her father had taught her too well. The added security wouldn't be enough to save the necklace.

Another quick glance around the room revealed a matched set of modern Danish chairs, and she silently pulled one in front of the portrait. Putting one foot on the seat, she rested her pack on her knee and retrieved a stethoscope, which she hung around her neck, a tube of gel, which she stuck up her sleeve, and another Cochard original: a telescoping mirror with a lever-action suction cup. She unwrapped the mirror from its cotton cloth and used a blow brush to whisk away all traces of lint. Seven minutes and counting.

Now came the hard part, and Chantal took an extra five seconds, rolling her fingers and emptying her mind of miscellaneous thoughts. But the memories she'd held at bay all night insisted on intruding: a rain-washed night in Monte Carlo, she and Paul running over the slate roof of the Dubois villa, high on excitement, eager to get home to their father and share their victory; then a shot.

Chantal's mental barriers came down with a clang. She wouldn't think of that night. She *couldn't* think of that night, or she'd be lost. She was alone and had a job to do, and with a determined twist of her fingers she anchored the mirror to the wall. Cupping the reflective surface in her palm, she slowly, very slowly, began interfacing the photoelectric beam with the mirror.

Before he attempted the impossible, Jaz decided to check out another route. Air Force Intelligence had certainly gone downhill since he'd been on the payroll. He slid down a valley in the roof and climbed up another eave. Rich people had such great roofs over their heads, he thought. This one was like the Rockies in miniature.

As he hung over the new edge his mood brightened. French doors, a small balcony, and the windows were dark. He only hoped it was still the library. In one fluid motion he slipped over the side and dropped to the balcony, landing with a soft thud.

He reached inside the pocket of his jean jacket and had a lockpick half out of its case before something incredibly strange registered in his brain—the French doors were already open. His gaze followed the gap up, and he caught the faint gleam of metal at the top.

Photoelectric beams are single-minded things. They only ask one question: Am I seeing the light? Chantal checked the angle between the mirror and the transmitter, knew the answer was yes, and carefully moved her hand away.

Releasing her pent-up breath, she swung the picture frame out from the wall. Every nerve was on red-line alert. If she'd made a mistake, her feet were ready to fly. One thousand one, one thousand two . . . She counted off the five-second lag time between a communication break and the alarm system. Nothing happened. Ten minutes down.

Jaz flattened his body against the gallery wall and peeked around the arch. A quick search of the moonlit room revealed his cointruder well into the business of getting into the safe. After a few moments he shook his head in pure admiration. There was nothing like watching a master at work. Figuring out how to sabotage a sophisticated security system was one thing, but being able to pull it off took a rare breed. And this lady was rare, not only in her skill and grace, but, he noted with an appreciative gleam, in every perfectly proportioned curve. There was no doubting the gender of this particular burglar.

Jumping into the middle of the delicate scene, he decided, was not the smartest course of action. He had some serious doubts about the jerry-rigged-mirror bit. Everybody had his own style, and some were equipment freaks and some weren't. He wasn't. Maybe it was better if he stayed close to the door.

With that problem neatly pigeonholed for the moment, Jaz settled in to watch the show. He leaned his shoulder against the arch and shoved his hands deep into the pockets of his dark slacks. A grin twitched the corner of his mouth. She was doing all the hard work for him. Another thought wiped the grin completely off his face. If she went for the stolen documents, he'd have to take her out. Gently, if possible, but he'd have to do it. One consolation, though, was that she didn't look big enough to give him any trouble.

Chantal squeezed a dab of gel onto the door of the safe, next to the combination lock, and stuck the stethoscope to it. That left both hands free and lessened the chance of her own heartbeats interfering. She opened her mouth the slightest bit to heighten her aural senses.

A good safecracker needed a number of things: good hearing, reliable instincts, and steady hands. A great safecracker added one more—a soft touch. Chantal had a very soft touch. She had inherited it from her father, Guy Cochard, and he from his father before him, and so on, down through the generations. She had been born into a family of thieves, proud thieves, who lived by their own defiant code: *The world is full of thieves. The Cochards are just honest about it, and they are the best.*

As a child Chantal had believed every word of that code, and only a disastrous twist of fate had changed the course of her life and shown her another world. A world where her family members were revealed for what they were—thieves, plain and simple. The lesson had been hard learned, the guilt a heavy burden, and her love for them a heavier burden still.

Being honest and being the best were values Chantal continued to hold dear, but she'd given up the thief part a long time ago, on a sad and rainy night in Monaco.

Or she'd believed she'd given it up, she thought, sighing heavily. The tumblers rolled and fell into place—left, right, left. Victory was at hand. She pulled down the handle and the door swung open.

"Excuse me," Jaz said.

Excuse me? What in the hell! Chantal's mental clock went haywire, the minute hand whirled, the springs twanged, and her whole world fell down around her ears. But she didn't move a muscle; she didn't even twitch.

"Don't panic," Jaz continued, "but as long as you're in there, could I get a few things?"

Things? He wants to get a few things? The bizarre question raced around her mind on wings of panic. She forced a breath from her lungs and slowly twisted her torso around, every nerve pulsing danger from one end of her body to the other. She spotted him instantly, a lanky figure in black lounging against the gallery arch.

Her tongue twisted in acrobatic flips. She had to say something, do something. "Who are you?" she finally croaked out.

"Jaz Peterson."

Good Lord! The man had given her his name! Was he crazy? She certainly wasn't going to return the favor. "What are you doing here?" She knew that was a pretty high-handed question for someone in her position, but she didn't know what else to say.

"I'm here to break the safe, but you seem to have everything under control. Please continue." When she didn't move, he added, "I'm not the cops, really. As long as we're not after the same thing, we should get along just fine."

"And exactly what are you after?" *For the love of God! Was this conversation really taking place?*

"Stolen government documents. How about you?" His voice was deep and soothing, his tone ridiculously casual, considering the situation, but his steady calm seeped through her fear, and she felt her heart slow down a half a beat from sheer panic.

"I'm—I'm only after what is mine," she stammered.

"Well, I know my papers don't belong to you, so we shouldn't have any problems. Seems like Sandhurst likes to acquire a lot of things that don't belong to him."

"He's in that business," she agreed carefully, her eyes straining across the dim interior to keep him in view.

"Do you need some help?" Jaz pushed himself off the arch and began a slow walk toward her. He didn't want to frighten her; the mirror getup was mere inches from her shoulder. But neither did he want her closing up shop before he got what he'd come for.

"No, I . . . uh, work better alone," Chantal said. She had been stretching her intuition and instincts to the maximum, searching for a source of danger in the stranger. Surprisingly, she found none. Time was tight. If he wasn't going to blow the whistle or attack her, she had to dismiss him and get on with her business.

She expelled another long breath before turning back to the safe, not wanting her nerves to make her careless. This was still a very delicate business. Her hand reached for the velvet jewelry case and eased it out of the safe. She snapped open the lid, checked the contents, and slipped it into her pack. Before she could swing the door shut, though, his hand slid up her arm.

"Honest," he whispered, "this will only take a second." He stuck a glowing penlight in his mouth, then pulled a sheaf of papers out of the safe and thumbed through them. Every action was efficient, no move wasted, and in less than a minute he had found what he wanted and put the remaining papers back inside. The light disappeared in his pocket. "Thanks."

There was a smile in his voice, one she saw reflected in the moonlight as his mouth widened in a sheepish grin. He pulled his sweater out of his pants and tucked the documents inside the waistband. "I really appreciate your help. . . ."

Was he crazy?

". . . I'm not sure I could have handled the system all the way. I was ready for the safe, but the high-tech business was more than I'd counted on."

The knot in her stomach grew to an unmanageable size, having as much to do with guilt as fear that they'd both get caught. She had to get out of there.

"You're really good," he continued. "I got here in time for the show, and I'm—"

"Will you shut up?" she hissed. Her mind was

going eight beats to the measure, and Mr. Run-on Mouth wasn't helping. She went into action, undoing the tracks of her entry, pushing the safe shut and spinning the lock. In thirty seconds it would be time to put the transmitter back in connection with its original receiver, and she sent up another prayer.

"Back off," she commanded the stranger, sending him a quelling look. "This is tricky, and I don't want you—"

"—screwing it up," he finished for her. "Be my guest."

Criminy, he's polite for a cat burglar! she thought. Flexing her fingers, she took another deep breath and tried, unsuccessfully, to block him from her mind. She reached for the mirror. A tremor vibrated the delicate instrument.

Letting out a heavy sigh, she removed her hands and shook them. Her palms were sweating, a bad sign. Another deep inhale and she reached again, holding her breath as she bent her fingers into a cradle.

With great care she began easing the mirror from beneath the transmitter. Her mind counted off each second of success. Seven . . . eight . . . nine . . . Nerves of steel snapped at nine. The mirror slipped in her sweat-dampened glove, flashing black, then silver, and black again as it twisted into disaster.

"Damn." The curse was a plaintive whisper.

She grabbed the mirror, ripped it off the wall, and hit the floor at a dead run, shoving her tools in her bag as she flew toward the French doors. Three . . . four . . . five. She tore through the doors and the alarm went off.

One hand pulled the magnets free, and she used the other one to loft herself onto the balcony rail.

Two large hands grabbed her thighs and boosted her to the roof as lights snapped on all around the mansion, flooding the darkness into day. The raucous clanging of the alarm system screamed through her ears and richocheted around her brain.

They raced across the roof, but when Chantal would have gone one way and Jaz another, he grabbed the waistband of her slacks and jerked her toward the cliff side of the house. She wasn't going to waste time arguing.

Halfway over the last peak a shotgun blast froze them both in their tracks. An instant later Jaz bodily threw himself over her and rolled them both into a valley of the roof.

Short breaths mixed in a cloud of vapor. Hearts pounded together beneath their black sweaters.

"Damn," she whispered, trying to control the wave of déjà vu threatening to paralyze her. The die for disaster had been cast ten years ago. She should have known better than to try to right a wrong with a wrong.

"You got that right," Jaz muttered. If he hadn't been a gentleman he would have added a few more descriptive phrases. He wasn't cut out for this. What in the world had General Moore been thinking? And why in the hell had he allowed himself to be shanghaied into this disaster? Piece of cake, the general had said. That should have been a clue, Jaz, old boy, he told himself. The azure waters and warm sandy beaches of the Caribbean were looking mighty far away right now. All he had was a frozen roof, a group of trigger-happy vigilantes lying in wait, and one very intriguing woman cushioning his body. Maybe things weren't as bad as he thought.

He raised his head to get a better look at her.

Heavy flakes of snow had landed on her grime-streaked face and rested lightly on her eyelashes. The blackface smudged her features, outlining a pair of wild eyes, the pupils blocking out all but a rim of pale luminosity. Her small breasts rose and fell in a staccato rhythm, pressing against his chest on every other beat.

Fear was a contagious beast, and it was rolling off this lady. Jaz decided a distraction was in order. "You never told me your name," he said close to her ear.

Chantal's eyes widened even more, and her body stiffened. "You got that right." She threw his words back at him, amazement blocking her panic. Who was this guy? she wondered, but she didn't ask. She had a sneaky suspicion he would probably tell her, and she didn't want to know. The less she knew the better.

Three more shotgun blasts came in quick succession, and with each one Jaz wrapped her more tightly in his arms, throwing his leg over hers and burying his head in the crook of her neck. She flinched with each explosion, her hands digging deeper into the sweater underneath his jacket. She didn't know how her hands had gotten that close to him, but she wasn't about to let go. His muscles were like whipcord beneath her fingers. Even through her fear she felt the strength of his arms protecting her, the warmth of his breath on her skin, and she wondered at the strangeness of her thoughts.

The last shot faded into the more powerful sound of the alarm, and she felt his mouth move over her ear again.

"I beg your pardon?" she asked, not believing what she'd heard.

"You smell good." That got her attention, he

thought, and she *did* smell good, soft and womanly. The scent and feel of her teased his mind with a memory he couldn't quite place.

"At a hundred and fifty an ounce, I should smell good," she snapped. Her aunt Elise always bought the most extravagant gifts. Oh, brother, why did she have to think of her aunt now? Elise would be mortified if she knew what her one and only niece was doing. Not worried, because she was well aware of the depth of the Cochard skill, but just mortified, because she'd never expected those skills to be used on her side of the world.

Lord, Chantal thought, she wished he would quit breathing in her ear. It was very distracting. Distracting and warm, and she wondered if she was on the verge of hysterics. She couldn't think of any other reason for her mind to be so bent on straying when she needed every atom of her body to survive. She'd never had this problem before. Concentration was her forte.

"Real good," Jaz went on. His leg tightened around hers, drawing her closer. "Too good to pass up," he drawled huskily, moving his mouth over hers.

What was he doing now? Her mouth opened in protest, but the words died on her lips, taken away with her breath when he deepened the kiss. His tongue delved into her mouth, and a frisson of pure electricity froze her motionless beneath him. Sometime in the next two minutes Chantal learned two things: Kissing a stranger had an incredible effect on her, and a kiss could block out reality. It wasn't the silence that warned her the alarm had been turned off; it was the sound of agitated voices coming from the lawn.

Jaz lifted his head and gently brushed his thumb over her cheek, tracing the curve to her brow. Chantal focused on the shadowed depths of the eyes so close to hers and slowly surfaced from a cloud of confusion. Unconsciously she ran her tongue over her lips, still warm from his kiss. Who was this guy? The thought was persistent, but she refused to give it priority. She didn't want to dwell on the powerful effect of his kiss. It didn't make sense.

"I've got to get out of here," she whispered, barely gathering the energy to shove him away.

"Me too," he said, and she would have sworn she saw the flash of a smile behind his blackface.

Shaking herself free from his mesmerizing gaze, she rolled onto her feet and hazarded a glance over the peak. The first thing she realized was that she couldn't go down the way she had come up. The second was that she could very well be trapped on the roof. Voices were coming from three sides of the house and she knew the fourth side was a seventy-foot drop over a cliff. Anger tightened her small hands into fists. She was going to kill this jerk for messing her up, no matter how well he kissed. She should hit him for that anyway.

"You low-down . . ." She didn't get any further before he grabbed her hand and hauled her over the peak. "Let go of me, you . . . "

He only moved faster, his grip tightening. Was she never going to get a word in? she wondered, taking two steps for each of his, all of them against her will. The strength that had protected her was now dragging her toward her doom. She was sure of it.

He stopped a few feet from the expansive library window and dropped to his knees. She followed suit and was gearing up to light into him again when she saw the fluid action of a rope snake out of his hands over the edge. A man with a plan.

Hope flickered back to life, and she shot him a quick glance. She had done some rappelling before, and although she was by no means an expert, she knew enough. The principle, at least, was simple. The rappeller, safe in a harness, held onto the rope with two hands, one in front of him, the other at his hip. The rope was threaded through a metal figure eight, which provided the necessary friction. Slackening off on the rope allowed it to slide; tightening on it kept it from running.

He threw her the harness and she stepped into the webbed loops, jerking on the rope to double-check the anchor. A clip of the carabiner into the figure eight and she was ready.

Before the word *go* was out of his mouth, she was over the edge and rappelling herself with world-record speed into the safety of darkness. Her feet tapped the window and she pushed off again, letting the rope zing through her hands. She landed in a tangle at the bottom of the cliff. Her mind was beyond fear, and with methodical speed she relieved herself of the harness and tugged on the rope. He was on his own now.

She spun around and started her dash for freedom, but didn't get five yards before a large square of light brightened the shadows at her feet. She whirled back, dropping to a crouch as her eyes quickly scanned the awful scene behind her. The library light had flashed on, creating an obscenely large backdrop for the lone figure coming down the back of the house. Even though Chantal knew she should keep running, her body didn't budge.

"Let it out," she muttered. "Come on, go for it." Her eyes were glued to the lanky silhouette. She wasn't even aware of her whispered encouragement, or of the cold creeping up around her ankles into her legs, or of the blood oozing from the rope burns across her palms.

One jump and two or three more feet and he would be past the window. She held her breath, unconsciously rising and stepping toward the cliff. As soon as he was clear she'd run like hell. Then the nightmare of her memories unfolded.

Both barrels of a shotgun exploded, shattering glass into confetti. Chantal instinctively dove for the rope and buried her head between her shoulders—but not before seeing Jaz slump against the wall.

Two

Glass fell in a brittle shower from the winter sky, and Chantal hid farther under her arm, praying for the cruel rain to stop. *Paul, Paul.* The name flooded her mind with images, dragging a sob from deep in her chest.

In seconds it was over and reality took hold. There had been no rope in Monaco, no cliff, no bite of cold numbing her fingers. Slowly she raised her head, and found Jaz halfway up the cliff, twisting and turning in the rope, his body dangling at a dangerous angle. *Get out of here!* The warning flashed across her brain. But there was another message, a stronger message battling in her heaving breast: *Help him.* Without her belay, the rope would flow like water through his harness connection and he'd drop like a stone. Once she had run. She couldn't do it again.

Using her weight, she tightened the friction on the figure eight to give him a chance, his only chance. "I've got you! Rap down!" Her voice echoed hollow and high off the cliff wall. He twisted again, and the rope jerked her off the ground. Chantal gasped for breath and squeezed her eyes shut, pulling for his life, her muscles wrapping around each other until they hurt.

She touched earth and spread and braced her feet against a fallen tree, hanging like a hundred pounds of deadweight on the end. "Move! Jaz!" Her scream teetered on the edge of panic.

Jaz was in trouble. He knew it as sure as he was hanging there. He had lost the rope out of one hand and his ears were ringing in two octaves. Cold, rough stone bit into his cheek. At least he'd had enough sense to slide past the window, but where was the rope? Like an answer to his prayers, the rope tightened with a jerk and he swung upright.

A voice cut through the buzzing in his head. *Move*, it commanded, and Jaz did his damnedest to obey. He reached out for the rope, but a sharp pain lanced him from his shoulder to his neck and down his arm, cramping his fingers into an ineffectual fist. The ringing in his ears increased, and somewhere, way in the back of his mind, he wondered if this was the end of the line.

"Move! Move, you crazy sonofa—Move, Jaz!" The harsh cry came again from below, lighting a fire under his survival instincts.

Ignoring the pain, he clenched the rope with a white-knuckled grip and immediately felt her slack off. *No place to go now but down, Jaz, old boy, and fast.* The thought and action were simultaneous as he slipped down the rope, yards at a time, his body burning. At the bottom, a pair of strong, supple arms came around his waist, pulling him off the rope and supporting his weight.

"Thanks. Ah . . ." He winced when she tucked her shoulder under his arm, but just feeling the ground beneath his feet sent a fresh wave of strength through him.

"You're hurt," she said with a gasp, and he

lightened his weight on her body. She was so small, he wondered if he'd been kissing jailbait. He hoped not, because he wanted to kiss her again. Planned on it, actually, his previous lightly embarked-upon distraction having turned into a lingering exploration of surprisingly sensual delight.

"It's just a flesh wound," he said bravely. Lord, he hoped it was just a flesh wound, but what he knew about wounds would fit on the head of a pin. It hurt like hell. That he knew for sure.

"We've got to get out of here."

"I'm game. What's the plan?"

"Don't *you* have a plan?" What had she gotten herself into?

"I've got a snowmobile."

"Where?"

"Half a mile to the north."

"Can you walk?"

"Yes." Jaz tested his knees to see if the fear-induced jelly had hardened up yet.

Her eyes met his for an instant, sharp and intense. "Then run."

Chantal took her own advice, racing over the forest rubble to the end of the ravine. He either made it now or he was on his own, she told herself. But he stuck to her like glue, his hands grabbing for branches she had barely cleared. When they scrambled to the top of the gulch, it was his hand stopping her backslide, his hand on her instep giving her the final boost over the top.

Chantal scrambled to her feet and steadied herself in the drifting snow; then she reached down for his hand. He was already halfway up, and her added tug sent him flying over the edge. A tangle of arms, legs, and bodies ensued, with Jaz gaining the high ground. The breath whooshed out of her lungs.

"Sorry," he grunted, without making the effort to move.

She knew he was hurting. It showed in the awkward angle of his arm between their stomachs and his labored gasps filling the air with vapor clouds. She'd give him five seconds, and not a moment more.

"It's okay," she said. "Uh . . . good-bye and good luck." Like their previous conversations, her statement sounded ridiculous, especially with him sprawled all over her, pressing her into the snow.

He groaned in answer and levered himself up on one elbow. Light from the full moon spilled onto his face, delineating the square line of his jaw and the curve of his cheekbones up to his eyes. The rest of his face remained a mystery, and for the first time Chantal allowed herself to wonder what he looked like. But his five seconds were up.

"We've got to get out of here." She started to slide from beneath him.

"Can I give you a ride home?"

The line was so out of place, she couldn't stop a smile from curving her mouth. "I don't think so." The roar of a snowmobile engine in the distance instantly changed her mind. "Maybe that's not such a bad idea." She'd never be able to outski a snowmobile.

"Let's go." His words bespoke haste; his actions didn't. Slowly and carefully he rolled off her and into the snow. One arm was held close to his waist as he stood. He used the other to grasp her forearm and hold her steady until she got her feet under her.

"I've got to pick up my skis," she informed him, stopping herself from brushing off the snow clinging to her clothes. In this light, the more mottled her coloring the better. She noticed he left the snow on his clothes too.

"Lead on." He graciously stepped back and let her break the trail.

She took a couple of seconds to get her bearings before striking off into the forest. The moon was both a blessing and a danger as they melted into the shadows, loping from tree to tree, from light into darkness and back again. Five minutes later they found her cache. A troop of snomobiles was crisscrossing the Sandhurst property in wide sweeps, the arcs of the headlights slicing through the night and bouncing off the trees. The whine of the engines rose and fell with the landscape.

Chantal strapped on her skis, and Jaz threw her pack over his good shoulder. Silently he signaled her to wait, the pressure of his hand on her shoulder all the warning she needed. A snowmobile roared past them less than twenty yards away, the closest yet. When it headed off into the night, he tapped her on the arm and Chantal took off. Her instincts were to give it everything she had and fly up the trail, but she forced herself to a slower pace, knowing if she lost him her best chance for getting out of there would also be lost.

The trek from her cache to the snowmobile took them farther and farther from her original route, and her confidence wavered with each added yard. Following a stranger into nowhere hadn't been a part of her plan. But it wasn't really nowhere, she reminded herself. No matter where they ended up, she could find her way home. An innate sense of direction and at least a passing familiarity with any stretch of the countryside were her guarantees against ever being lost in these mountains. And she could ski all night if she had to.

Jaz stumbled on the trail, and she sliced her skis into the snow to keep from plowing into him.

Before she could lend a helping hand, he was up and moving again. Could he make it? If he was a flatlander, the altitude alone had already cut his stamina in half. Would she continue putting herself in danger if he really couldn't make it?

Questions, questions. She hated the questions, was unsure of the answers. Kicking off with an angry burst of energy, she caught up to him with three long glides and stayed close, until he stopped by an outcropping of granite. The huge boulder jutted into the night sky, shadowing the land beneath it and the snowmobile. Relief flooded through her, washing away the little shreds of guilt nagging at her conscience. Of course they were going to make it, and no, she wouldn't have left him if he hadn't been able to keep up.

While she stepped out of her skis, he straddled the seat. But when he reached for the key, she grasped his hand.

"The second you start this thing, they're going to know exactly where we are. Let me drive. I know where we're going."

The words were more of a command than a request, which didn't seem to faze him. He cocked his head and flashed her a grin, the last thing she'd expected, considering their grueling hike. "You crack a damn good safe, lady, but trust me, I can outdrive anybody in these hills tonight. You just hold on and point and I'll get us there."

His easy confidence told her he wasn't bluffing, and for the second time Chantal wondered what he looked like beneath the blackface and knit cap. She sure liked his smile. She didn't even want to think about his kiss. "How's your shoulder?"

"It hurts." He flexed his fingers, testing them out. "But I'm scared enough to overlook it until we're out of here."

His admission surprised her. For some inexplicable reason, she was tuned in to this stranger. As she hadn't found danger before, she didn't find fear now—only a dauntless optimism strong enough to diminish her own too-real fears.

She bundled her skis under her right arm and used her left to hold on, curling her fingers tightly around the front of his waistband. Her fingers pressed into the taut muscles of his stomach, but intimacy never crossed her mind. If he was going to get them out of there it was going to be a wild ride, and she wasn't going to get dumped. When Jaz turned the key, the engine roared to life like a jet engine, the sound and the power almost blowing her off the seat.

Taken completely by surprise, she hollered, "What kind of snowmobile is this?"

He flashed her another grin over his shoulder. "Turbo-charged." Then he gunned the motor and they took off like an earthbound rocket.

Just as Chantal had predicted, the other snowmobiles coalesced into a beeline headed straight for them, but there was no catching Jaz's machine. They raced on the edge of danger and disaster. For all their speed and recklessness, she never felt that he was out of control or that they had a snowball's chance in hell of losing their pursuers. Sandhurst's men fell farther behind, but Jaz was laying a line of tracks a blind man could have followed.

What had she been thinking when she'd cast her lot with the snowmobile instead of her silent cross-country skis? she asked herself. Her plan had been to hook up with one of the many ski trails crisscrossing the countryside. Their pursuers never would have been able to distinguish her tracks from the others, but then again, she never would have made it to the trails in time. Sandhurst would have had her skinned and hung out to dry less than a mile from the mansion.

Jaz took them up over a rise, and the snowmobile caught air at the top. Chantal held on for dear life, her grip tightening on everything that was grippable, his sweater, his pants, maybe even a part of him that under different circumstances would have shocked her. The sharp edges of her bindings cut into her upper arm, and the driven snow beat against one of her frozen cheeks. The other was buried in the worn softness of his denim jacket.

Five miles from the Sandhurst mansion, she directed him onto the Forest Service trail that switchbacked across the mountainous terrain to within a couple of miles of her cabin. The snowmobile rocked on the treacherous turns, with Chantal making herself a shadow of his every move, leaning out from the curves to keep the skids on the snow. She doubted if another snowmobile had ever attempted the trail, and she wondered about the wisdom of doing it now. Jaz didn't seem to harbor the same worries. He not only kept the snowmobile upright, but added to the thrill by taking a few shortcuts that jammed her heart up into her throat. The man could drive, of that she was sure. Everything else was up for grabs. They needed a plan.

Suddenly Jaz pulled off the trail and tore through a stand of aspens. Chantal jerked frantically on his jacket, trying to direct him back down the mountain. Thirty yards into nowhere, he came to a stop and turned off the machine.

Muttered curses floated through the air.

"What in the hell do you think you're doing?"

"Where in the hell are you taking us?"

They both swung their legs over the snowmobile and squared off.

"Dammit, I'm the one giving directions."

"Around and around and around. We're getting nowhere fast."

"Nowhere is right. We need to go thataway," she said urgently, pointing her finger down the mountain in quick jabbing motions.

Jaz grabbed her hand, his grip firm but not painful. "Lady, what we need is a plan. In case you haven't noticed—"

The crack and echo of a rifle shot stopped the conversation cold and sent them both diving behind the snowmobile. Jaz still held her hand, and as she vainly tried to free herself she lapsed into a stream of French profanity, most of it directed at him.

"I resent that," he whispered through clenched teeth.

Oh, brother. "You speak French?"

"Only the kind you do. I can't get through a menu."

"Well, *I* can."

Jaz whipped her around, and their knees bumped. "Great. Congratulations." He craned his head forward until their noses almost touched, his voice rising with each syllable. "But can you get us the hell out of here?"

Another rifle shot cracked in the distance, and Jaz jerked her into his lap with one powerful move, using his body as a barrier between her and the unseen death strafing the night. Seconds ticked by with nothing but the sound of the snow falling through the trees and the creak and groan of frozen boughs dipping in the wintery breeze.

Jaz slowly raised his head above the vinyl seat of the snowmobile, listening and waiting.

"I can't breathe," Chantal mumbled into the tensely muscled thigh pressed against her face. Everything about his body was tight, hard, masculine. She must be losing her mind, she thought, thoroughly flustered by her awareness of him.

"Shh." His hand cupped the back of her neck, gently holding her where she lay. The far-off whine of engines was a discordant backdrop to the silence of nature. "Who are they shooting at? They've got to be at least a mile away."

"Us, big boy," Chantal answered with an exasperated sigh, fighting her way clear of his arms. Her hand dug into his sweater for leverage. As she straightened she felt a stickiness on her fingers through the frayed ends of her gloves. Sweat was running off both of them, despite the temperature, but the viscous fluid she rubbed between her thumb and index finger wasn't sweat. Dawning recognition sent a shiver of fear down her spine. "You're bleeding. A lot. My God, Jaz."

"That's not exactly a news flash," he retorted. Then he caught the concern shining in her eyes, the paleness of her skin beneath the hastily applied grime, and he reached out and touched her face. "Hey, it's okay. I'm not dead yet." His thumb brushed across her cheek and tucked a strand of golden hair back under her cap. Her hair was soft, vibrant; her skin cold and softer still. Reassuring her increased his own confidence past practical bounds. "We need a plan, and, believe it or not, I've got one. How far are we from where you want to be?"

"My cabin is about two miles from here, mostly downhill."

"Where?"

Chantal hesitated, her gaze dropping to where she had wiped his blood on her pants.

Jaz understood, but he knew his options had dwindled desperately since he'd taken her on. "I'll be honest with you. I'm lost, and I'll never outrun them all night. Hell, I'll probably freeze to death before dawn . . . or you can save me. Let me stay with you, if I make it."

"I'm not exactly home free," she reminded him.

"You will be in about thirty seconds. If you're half as fast as I think you are, I can hold them off long enough for you to get home."

"And if I don't tell you where I live?"

He shook his head and smiled at her, a band of white in his darkened face. "Lady, you're out of here either way. But if you say no, I'm gonna miss you." And he would, he thought, that was the amazing thing. Sometime during their mad dash he'd made a vow—if nothing else, before this was over he'd know what she looked like, this woman who'd saved him, this woman whose kiss had pulled such an unexpected response from him.

Chantal realized the depth of his need, knew she was the only chance he had. For whatever reasons, for this one night her life was entwined with a stranger's—and she wanted him to survive.

She didn't give herself time to change her mind, and quickly gave him directions. "The last switch-back empties out into a meadow. A quarter of a mile south of there, there's a cut in the mountains to the west. It leads into a larger valley, and my cabin is on the north side, about halfway up the hill." She prayed she hadn't just made the biggest mistake of her life. Second biggest, actually, the first having been being born a Cochard, a heritage she seemed incapable of avoiding. Ten years on her own, five as a successful real-estate agent, and she still felt the call of duty and the weight of a debt unpaid.

"Thanks. One more question." She noticed him flinch as he rolled his good shoulder to ease the pain of the bad one. She too was feeling the aches and scrapes of their escape, and the cold of the night was becoming an uncomfortable reality. "What is your name?"

THIEVES IN THE NIGHT • 33

Why not? she thought. It was too late for that bit of information to protect her. "Chantal Cochard," she said.

"Shan-tal Co-shard." He drawled her name slowly, letting it sit on his tongue. A mischievous glint warmed his eyes as he repeated her name and bent from the waist to lower his head close to hers. His mouth was only a breath away. "Thank you, Chantal." His cool lips brushed across hers, the two mouths together kindling a flame.

He used his good hand to cup her face, his touch warming her there also. Gently he traced her lips, and she felt herself sink inside, wondering again at the delight of kissing a stranger. Was that fate whispering in her ear?

Of its own volition her hand raised to his face, her fingers discovering the roughness of his jaw, the arc of his cheekbone, and the softness of his eyebrow. Her hand came to rest on his cheek, and she felt the muscle there curve into her palm. A new sense of wonder warmed her from the inside out; she'd never been kissed with a smile before. Her lips parted.

Jaz slid his hand to her nape and turned her deeper into the kiss. Like a dying man taking his last breath, he opened his mouth over hers, taking every ounce of sweetness she gave. The smile faded from his face, replaced by a hint of desperation.

Chantal clung to him, savoring the taste of him and the heat coursing through his veins. Flame turned to fire under the breathless track of his tongue. Another rifle shot froze them both in mid-kiss.

"Take these," he whispered between short kisses. "Ah, damn." His open mouth twisted over her lips.

She felt his wince as much as she heard it.

Then he was shoving his papers down her pants and under her sweater. They were still warm from his body.

"Washington, D.C., General Moore. Remember that my name's Jaz Peterson." One more complete kiss that left her feeling strangely incomplete. "Good luck." He pulled her to her feet and helped her snap into her skis.

"Jaz." Reluctance made her voice ragged. She reached out to touch his waist, but she was already sawing grooves into the snow with her skis.

He slipped his hand in hers. "Partners?" he asked.

Unfathomably pleased that they had put some kind of label on their tenuous relationship, she gave his hand a solid shake. "Partners."

"Then go, Chantal. Ski like a pack of wolves is on your tail."

She squeezed his hand one last time and pushed off. In less than a minute she had done a telemark on the switchback and disappeared into the shadows.

Jaz got to work, checking to make sure the gas tank was on the leeward side. A Swiss Army knife and a bandanna came out of his pocket, and he began cutting the cloth into two-inch strips. When they were knotted together, he stuffed one end in the gas tank and trailed the rest down the side of the snowmobile.

Searching the outskirts of the aspen glade, he found the perfect obstruction, a pair of downed lodgepole pines almost bare of branches. A flash of light to the south lengthened his strides and brought renewed strength to his arms. Sandhurst's men were starting the switchbacks at the top of the mountain.

He felt the wound on his shoulder gape and bleed afresh as he dragged the trees across a bend in the trail, propping one on top of the other and anchoring their bushy tops together. Three more lights joined the one crisscrossing the trail.

Legs pumping, heart pounding, he raced back to the snowmobile. His first match was extinguished before the cloth lit; his hands started shaking.

"Come on, honey, don't let me down," he whispered. The second match took, but the flame didn't hold past the first knot. "Dammit, there goes my safety net."

Frantic now, he shoved the rest of the bandanna down the gas tank and pulled it out soaking wet. The crash, whine, and hollering of a snowmobile plowing into the barrier of trees jumbled up the night with confusion and sound. Jaz struck another match close to the cloth.

And then he ran like hell.

Arms and legs working in tandem, Chantal worked her way to the top of the last rise before the cut through the mountains. Her muscles were trembling, screaming for her to slow down. She ignored them. She stretched her right leg sideways and lifted her left ski an inch off the ground for a massive push-off down the other side, but a sky-rocking explosion sent her into a slicing hockey stop.

The skis dug into the snow, throwing her around. She caught herself with a hard plant of her poles and stared wide eyed, her jaw slackening in shock.

Her knees knocked together in fear and coldness. Her eyes saw the winding dance of lights closing in on the plume of orange flame and black smoke. But her heart held only one word—Jaz.

Her gut knotted in agony, and she clutched her

stomach, feeling his papers. *Washington, D.C., General Moore. Remember that my name is Jaz Peterson.* She had no choice. *Partners.* An incredible wave of sadness lodged in her throat and shortened her breath as she pushed off into the moonlit night.

The closer she got to home, the more her emotions overrode her physical sense of reality. Her muscles refused to work, and her mind was too caught up in shock to make them do her bidding. The ski tips crossed again and again, bringing her to her knees with arms too shaky to continue pushing her upright.

The lights of the Palmer place were the first milestone. Her own yard light beckoned a quarter of a mile up the valley.

Kick, glide. Kick, glide. The litany ran through her mind until her hand gripped the stair rail leading to her deck. She stumbled up the steps, her boots sliding on the boards, the frayed ends of her gloves allowing snow to bite into her numb fingertips.

She pushed the door open and warm air rushed around her. The door closed behind her and she collapsed into a sobbing heap on the braided entry rug. Sadness, horror, and fear engulfed her senses, all for a man she didn't know. For generations of Cochards theft had been a game, a battle of wits without consequences. But as she had the night in Monte Carlo, Chantal felt the consequences of this night to the marrow of her bones.

Curled in a fetal position, she pulled off her cap and pressed it close to her mouth to muffle her sobs. A tangle of long blond hair fell around her face and soaked up the salty tears.

When the trembling of her limbs took on gargantuan proportions, she finally acknowledged what her body had been telling her for an hour; it needed care. She forced herself up onto rubbery legs and walked in a daze to the bathroom. Soon she was slipping into a tub of steaming water, sliding deeper and deeper, until only her face floated above the burning heat.

Jaz collapsed on the top of a rise and lay still. A web of pain spread from his shoulder through the length and breadth of his body. Squeezing his eyes shut, he started to count to ten, promising to get up somewhere between eight and nine. At eight he rolled over and drew his legs beneath his torso. At nine he fell back into the snow.

Don't do this to yourself, Jaz. Get up . . . get up . . . get up. He held the thought, tightly.

Opening his eyes, he stretched his neck back until he could see over the top of the rise. The cut Chantal had told him about started a few yards from the bottom of the hill. He brought his chin back to his chest and searched the switchbacks. Lights still bounced through the trees, but the snowmobile fire was dying.

Just like you will if you don't get up.

He rolled back onto his knees and willed his legs to hold him. Cradling his throbbing arm, he half ran, half fell, down the hill.

Three

Chantal sat on the edge of the bargello-upholstered wing chair in front of the fireplace, her eyes glued to the grandfather clock on the other side of the one-room cabin. A wood fire filled the home with warmth, from her living and kitchen area, to the raised dais holding her mahogany four-poster and armoire. The cabin was small, eight hundred square feet of hardwood floors and soft pine paneling, with large windows on the south, west, and east walls. Rugs of various styles were scattered around the room, and an antique red velvet sofa paralleled the moss-rock hearth. Most of the furniture had come from her aunt, whose only motto was, "When the going gets tough, the tough go shopping." If Elise ever found out about tonight, Chantal thought, the merchants in Aspen would probably have a percentage rise in their gross income.

The clock chimed the half hour. Eleven-thirty.

She'd give Jaz until midnight, she decided, and then she was going after him. In the bathtub her mind had started working again, coming up with a lot of *maybes*. Maybe he was alive, maybe he was hurt, maybe he needed her. Maybe she was crazy.

The pendulum swung back and forth. Her toes curled deeper into the Chinese carpet in front of the fireplace. She lifted a warmed snifter of brandy to her lips, took a sip, and her gaze drifted to the amber liquid running down the inside of the glass. Memories glazed her eyes as the liquor pooled into the bottom of the snifter, into the past. . . .

"Drink this." Her father's voice was gruff with strain. He opened her fist and put the tumbler of brandy in her hand.

Rain lashed the small-paned windows of the French country home, matching the tears streaming down her face. Chantal gulped the brandy and swallowed hard. "Poppa, Paul made me leave." She choked the words out between short gasps for air. "I didn't want to leave him. He's hurt, Poppa, hurt and alone on the roof of the Dubois villa."

"No, Chantal, the police have picked him up by now. They will care for him. We can do nothing tonight without endangering your safety. When he doesn't come home in the morning, I will call. By then you will be gone." He gently cupped Chantal's chin in his hand and tilted her head up. Light from the kitchen lamp sparked in her silver-gold hair. "Where are the Dubois jewels?"

"Paul kept them. He wanted to throw them off my trail, but they'll know it was a two-man job." Chantal grasped her father's wrist, trying to pull some of his solid strength into her trembling body. "What will happen to him, Poppa?"

"Nothing." Her father's voice was low with conviction. "Paul will return the jewels and I will use my influence to convince the Duboises not to press charges. Their slate is not so clean that they cannot be convinced. None of our 'clients' is that clean." He released Chantal's chin and waved his hand through the air in a dismissive gesture. "No one in Monte Carlo is that clean, except the Royal Family, God bless them all. In a hundred years the Cochards have never touched the Royal jewels."

"And where will I go? Paris?"

"*Non, chérie.* You I will send to America, to your *tante* Elise, until this blows over. Paul I will disown, publicly, so the scandal does not interfere with our legitimate jewelry business. A few years will pass and all will be forgotten. It is the way of the world."

His confidence did little to ease Chantal's guilt. She shook her head slowly from side to side, hiccuping between sobs. "I am as guilty as my brother. He shouldn't have to take all the blame. He shouldn't have made me leave."

"Paul did the right thing, the honorable thing. And do not worry, Chantal. I won't let them keep my son locked up. There are favors to call in, debts to be repaid, and I will use them all to gain Paul's release. The world is full of thieves—Dubois or Cochard—on both sides of the law." He helped her to her feet and smothered her in a bear hug before sending her up the stairs. "Now you must do as I say. Go pack your things. I will call Elise."

The world is full of thieves. Chantal swallowed the last of her brandy and crossed the room for a refill. Her father was right about the thieves; he'd been wrong about everything else. The Duboises hadn't backed down from the charges, and Paul had gone to jail. He had never revealed the identity of his accomplice . . . and he had never written to Chantal. She had carried her burden of guilt without respite for ten years.

A few years will pass and all will be forgotten. The intimate circle of Monte Carlo's elite had not forgotten, and the Cochards' legitimate jewelry business had all but folded under their unspoken yet all-inclusive boycott. The final blow had come three months ago, when a group of thieves hitting the Côte d'Azur had cleaned the Cochards out.

The tears she thought she had controlled began again as she uncorked the top of the brandy bottle. What irony, her father had written, that he, the greatest jewel thief in all of Monte Carlo, should be ruined by other thieves. But Chantal knew fate when she saw it, and one night a few weeks ago in the Hotel Orleans she had seen it wrapped around Angela Sandhurst's neck. *The world is full of thieves.*

Her father was overdrawn, underinsured, and he and Paul were on the brink of bankruptcy. Her brother's sacrifice and her father's belief and money had given Chantal a fresh start, a new direction in life. She could offer them no less. She didn't have the kind of money they needed, but they had given her something that she had never lost—their skill.

She hadn't been surprised to find her father's best piece hanging from the neck of Aspen's newest citizen. The older she got the smaller the world became, especially the world of the rich and infamous. No, she hadn't been surprised by that. But Jaz Peterson . . . Ah, yes, Jaz. In his presence she had felt the hand of fate grasping her shoulder. His kiss had only tightened the grip.

With the back of her hand she wiped the tears from her face and glanced at the clock. It struck midnight, and chimes filled the room.

• • •

Jaz huddled in the doorway, shaking with cold. Gusts of wind sent snow swirling around his body. *Please, sweet lady, please.* He closed his eyes and knocked again.

A wall of warmth rushed over his face as the door opened. Unfortunately he'd been using it to hold himself upright, and without the added support he tumbled into a heap at her feet.

"Damn!" He rolled onto his back to take the weight off his wounded shoulder. His knees were splayed, his right arm cradling his left one at the waist. Glancing up, he registered the wide-eyed shock and absolute, drop-dead gorgeousness of the woman staring down at him. "Ja-Jaz Peterson," he muttered, straining every syllable through chattering teeth. "Remember? You invited me."

"I remember," she said breathlessly, her sweetly feminine voice full of doubt. She clutched the door as if it were a life raft. Clouds of gold strayed from the pile of hair on top of her head. Tears tracked the high arch of her naturally blushed cheeks and pooled in the corners of her full mouth. Dark, almost black, eyebrows slanted above the bluest, wariest eyes he'd ever seen. He couldn't blame her. She was hardly seeing him at his best—a grime-streaked, shivering mass bleeding on her rug.

"Chantal, I'm freezing to death and I need to warm up . . . n-now. Have you got a bathtub?" Lord, he hated to think about how much that was going to hurt, but what was another level of pain added to the depth of hurt he was already feeling?

"Yes," she answered weakly.

It was a start, he thought, but it wasn't good enough. He needed help. Searching the depths of her guarded eyes, he sent out an emotional plea.

Help me, Chantal. Help me or I'm going to go into convulsions right here on your pretty hand-braided rug.

Something must have clicked in her mind, because she slammed the door shut and dropped to his side. "Put your arm around my waist." When he didn't respond, she did it for him, holding him close and taking a deep breath. Together they got him to his feet and stumbled into the bathroom.

Jaz huddled over her slender shoulders and used his forward momentum to step directly into the tub, clothes and all. Chantal stopped him before he sat down.

"This will just take a second," she said, putting one foot in the tub and wedging herself under his arm to keep him from falling over. She used both hands to jerk his pants down to his knees. "Okay."

His legs buckled, and he collapsed into the glossy black tub, dragging her with him. It was too late to stop the convulsions rippling through his body. *This is it, babe. Hold on tight.* He squeezed his eyes shut and clenched the back of her shirt, twisting the material into bunches, trying not to crush her in the spasmodic cramped circle of his arms.

Chantal responded without hesitation, wrapping her own arms around his shoulders and holding him for all she was worth. He'd survived the cliff, he'd survived the trail to her cabin. She'd be damned if she let him die in her bathtub.

His head twitched and jerked on her shoulder, and she grasped a hank of the thick brown hair falling over the collar of his jean jacket, holding him still until the shudder passed through his body into hers. His body was ice to her heat, hard angles to her softness, but the pulse of life beat heavily in his veins. She felt it in the bands of steel around her torso, in the force of the breath rasping against her neck.

Minutes passed, and she continued to hold him, her fingers soothing the chill from the tense column of his neck. Sliding her thumbs up his hairline, she laid her mouth on his ear and gauged the damage with her lips. Cold, but not frozen. He stirred at her touch, instinctively rubbing his ear against her mouth. The warmth of the room was slowly invading his limbs, slackening his aching grip on her body and easing his sharper pains of being alive. But it wasn't enough, and the pain wasn't as bad as it was going to get.

"Jaz. Help me," she pleaded, knowing they shouldn't wait any longer. She pushed the jacket off his shoulders. He released her shirt and buried his head deeper in the crook of her neck. As she drew the jacket down one arm, his mouth opened in a muffled groan and his teeth grazed her skin. His breath was warm and moist on the nape of her neck, and the full realization of the situation hit her like a thunderbolt. She tried to switch gears from mother nurturer to clinical helper, but he was so vulnerable, so in need of care and a tender touch.

She eased the jacket off the other arm and tossed it over the side of the tub to the floor. As gently as possible she released him and worked at getting his pants and chukka boots off, becoming aware for the first time of the length and strength of his legs. Lean muscles corded his thighs and knotted his calves under nut-brown skin, and she wondered how many days in the sun it took to acquire such a richly dark color. The hair on his legs was a sandy brown, and she automatically glanced at his head. Sun-bleached streaks wove through the dominant chestnut color. Many, many days in the sun, she decided.

His sweater was glued to his shoulder with his blood, and, knowing what was to come, she left it on. Time enough for that pain later. She started to climb out of the bathtub, but his fingers curling around her shirttail stopped her. His eyes were closed, and without her support, his head had slumped onto his shoulder.

"Don't go . . . please," he said weakly. Chantal's heart tightened in her throat, and she hesitated.

"Please," he begged again.

The night had been full of decisions more important than this one, she thought. She'd share this last pain with him. With a single action, she ripped open the snaps on her shirt and shrugged out of her suspenders. Her jeans fell in a heap, and she tossed her shirt onto the floor. Clad in a black T-shirt and black cotton panties, she stepped back in and pulled his feet into her lap. Empathy stayed her hand for a moment before she started the water gushing into the tub.

"Dear God . . ." His face contorted in pain, and a silent scream hissed through his bared teeth. He tried to jerk out of her grasp, but she held him tightly, her fingers strong and sure as she squeezed his toes and insteps.

"Shh . . ." she crooned softly in counterpoint to his labored groans, watching the heave and buck of his chest. The gasping sound tore at her heart. "Shh . . . you're okay. I know it hurts." She moved her hands up his calves, working magic with her fingers, helping him as much as she could.

She followed the rise of water up his body, rubbing and kneading his muscles back to life. Slowly his skin lost the icy paleness beneath the tan. Her knees were on either side of his, her hands massaging his thighs, when he pulled her down beside him, resting his head below her shoulder.

And she let him, holding him until the water threatened to overflow the tub.

Gently she extricated herself from his arms and leaned forward to turn off the faucets. Just as gently he brought her back. The sweater-covered arm around her waist slid her closer until his head once again rested in the valley between her breasts. His groans turned into heavy sighs.

The action surprised her. The strength of the action surprised her even more. This was not a man on the edge of death. At least she didn't think so.

"Jaz?"

"Hmmm." The answer came from deep in his throat, like a growl, or a purr.

"Are you okay?"

Slowly he tilted his head back, inadvertently smearing her T-shirt with blackface. Murky gray eyes caught hers with a languid gaze. "I'm not sure. Can we try this a little longer?" The words slurred over one another.

"Uh . . . sure." The first flush of modesty coursed up her neck and blushed her cheeks. She'd gotten herself into this, she thought, and she would tough it out. She hoped. Any doubts she had disappeared when she noticed the pink stain of his blood floating above their legs. He had to be hurting a lot more than his voice revealed.

"Great," he mumbled, snuggling back down, and she let them both rest, her eyes drifting shut in pure weariness. He would live.

The quarter hour slipped into the half hour and still she held him, feeling his chest press against hers in deep, even breaths. His thigh was now on top of hers and his arm had wrapped completely around her waist. Steam rose around them, dampening her face and wetting a few straying tendrils of hair against her cheeks.

The quiet and the warmth—and the man—drained the tension from her body. She was suffused with a sweet weakness that spread inward in soft spirals of pleasure. Seductive, melting pleasure . . .

Her eyes popped open and a low gasp escaped her lips. Her half-dead stranger was very much alive—alive and nuzzling her breast with his open mouth, kneading her through the thin cotton of her T-shirt.

"Jaz!"

Her cry went unheard. He bit down gently and ran his tongue across the peak. The spirals tightened and shot straight down her middle.

Oh . . . my . . . Lord.

"Jaz." She moaned, trying one more time to take control before she figuratively and literally sank.

Perplexed, glazed eyes lifted to hers. "Hi," he said softly. What he didn't say, but what she heard, was, "Who are you?"

"Jaz. If you're warm now, I think I should take care of your shoulder."

He nodded slowly, his eyebrows furrowing in confusion. "I'm plenty warm . . . real warm." His slate-gray eyes began to clear, and the faintest hint of a smile touched a corner of his mouth. "Even hot."

"Yes, well, then I'll just get what I—"

His fingers brushed across her lips, stopping her words. "Tell me one thing. Was I dreaming?"

Truth struggled with embarrassment, and won. "No," she admitted slowly. She couldn't have been in a more vulnerable or compromising position if she'd planned it.

"Then I apologize. Honest, Chantal, I thought I'd died and gone to heaven." The contrition in his eyes told her he wasn't lying. His simple confession of how she'd made him feel was something else entirely. She decided the most graceful way out of the situation was simple acceptance.

"It's okay, Jaz. We're both strung out." She untangled her body from his and stepped out of the tub.

He tried to follow, but the weight of the sodden sweater held him down. A wince flashed across his face. "You're going to have to cut this thing off me," he said. "It's killing my shoulder."

"I'll get a pair of scissors," she said, keeping her back to him as she padded around the room. At a hundred square feet, the bathroom doubled as a dressing area, easily accommodating a closet along one wall and her light-oak antique chiffonier. She grabbed dry undies, a towel, and her jeans and shirt. "I'll be right back."

In minutes she returned, fully clothed and holding the scissors in her hand. He'd let some of the water out of the tub, so only his legs were still covered.

"I thought I'd make it easier on us," he said, grinning through the rivers of blackface streaking his face. "If you cut up the sleeve, we should be able to pull it over my head without doing me in."

The camouflage was even more effective wet and runny, she thought, but somewhere underneath all that grime lurked a good, solid bone structure with everything in the right place and in the right proportion. Of course, a man didn't need much more of an edge than a smile like his, a mouth like his, and the expertise to meld them both into mind-numbing kisses. She was almost afraid to see what he really looked like.

"Okay," she replied, hoping she'd struck a casual note. She'd overcome the largest portion of her embarrassment in the living room, telling herself that if he'd thought he was dreaming he wouldn't really remember what had happened. But all she had to do was look into his teasing gray eyes to know she was only fooling herself. He remembered plenty.

"You seem to have bounced back pretty well," she continued in a light vein as she began cutting.

"Yeah, we Petersons are a tough breed." The closer she got to his shoulder, the narrower his gaze became, following each snip.

"Don't worry, Jaz, I've got steady hands. That slip-up at Sandhurst's was a rare occurrence," she said dryly, back on firm conversational ground.

His eyes fluttered open, the faint gesture an indication of his fatigue. "I trust you implicitly." A vaguely mocking smile twisted his mouth. "It's me I'm worried about."

She lifted a dark brow quizzically, but otherwise ignored his statement. Just as well, he thought. He didn't have the energy to explain the feelings she aroused. They were strong and tender, hotter than he'd confessed, and confusing him on more than one level.

Physically he understood his reaction. She was the prettiest, most delicately exotic woman he'd ever seen. A thoroughly mussed tumble of wild silver-blond hair was piled this way and that on top of her head, more than half of it falling around her shoulders. Her heart-shaped face and softly colored cheeks hinted at an innocence that belied her skill at Sandhurst's. Her eyes were like a newborn fawn's, soft and luminous, except bluer than a Colorado sky. Her skin looked like satin to touch. No, it didn't surprise him that he wanted to take her to bed. But it surprised the hell out of him that he wanted *her* to take *him* to bed.

She leaned in closer, unwittingly echoing his thoughts, filling his nostrils with her special scent, and an unconscious groan escaped him.

She immediately lightened her touch. "I'm sorry, Jaz, but I'm almost finished."

Her misinterpretation brought a wry smile to his mouth. And he was thinking about starting something she probably wouldn't let him finish even if he could. The electric response they'd shared in the heat of danger wasn't something he took for granted. When that much adrenaline was pounding through your blood, a person did a lot of things he wouldn't consider when he was safe at home. But they were far from safe even now, and he wondered if she knew it.

Wielding the scissors gently, Chantal cut through the neck of his sweater. "I'm going to take it off your other arm first; then we'll get it over your head. I'll try not to hurt you."

She didn't want to hurt him. The same maternal instincts she'd felt while she held him in the bathtub were at work now, cautioning her to be gentle. The other feelings she'd had when he had held her . . . Well, she was unsuccessfully trying to ignore those feelings.

She helped him slip his arm out of the intact sleeve and paused for a moment. "Are you ready?"

"Go for it." He gave her the thumbs-up.

She bundled the bulk of the sweater around his neck with both hands and as carefully as possible eased it over his head. A tremor jumped across his shoulder blades, but she didn't stop.

He pulled his head out from under the sweater and came up grinning. "We made it," he said, and sighed, slipping down and stretching full out in the tub.

The sheer cheerfulness of his smile warmed all the tender places of her heart. And the sight of his now nearly naked body turned those places to mush. No wonder he'd had the strength to hold

her when by all rights he should have been helpless, she thought. Sinewy muscles wrapped over
one another down the length of his arms, lean
and tight, like the muscles in his chest. His darkly
tanned skin stretched over the taut plane of his
stomach, taking a concave dive below his ribs.
Water lapped at the thin line of hair starting at
his navel and disappearing under the only article
of clothing she hadn't stripped off him, a pair of
black cotton running shorts. Wet, they didn't hide
much, and her heart flipped and sank.

"You got any soap, Chantal?" She snapped her
gaze up to his face. He pushed himself upright,
his eyes twinkling with an annoyingly accurate
summation of her thoughts.

"Yes. Sure," she said, giving herself a mental
shake and reaching behind her. She knew she
should leave now, before she made a complete
gaping fool of herself. But she didn't leave.

He soaped up the washcloth, and she watched
as the veins rose and receded along his biceps,
triceps, and every other muscle he had but she
couldn't name. Then he smeared the cloth over
his face and hair, turning the pink cotton into
gray. A small price to pay, she admitted when he
sluiced the soap off.

Boyishly handsome, despite the crow's feet feath-
ering the corners of his eyes, his face reflected all
the charm his smile had promised. His skin had
the same rich tan all over, except for the tip and
part of the bridge of his nose, which was peeling
to pink in spots. Too many days in the sun, she
decided. The dark curve of his cheekbones melded
into the darker hair of his eyebrows. His lashes
were even darker, thick and spiky with glittering
drops of water. In contrast his eyes were shifting
shades of gray, like a clear mountain stream. A
slight cleft dented his chin, and creases deepened

in his lean cheeks when he smiled—as he did
now.

"Well, what do you think?" His softly spoken
words jolted her out of her perusal.

"I . . . uh . . ." She lowered her eyes and scrambled mentally for something innocuous to say. "I
think I'll let you finish up alone. Are you hungry?"

His smile told her she hadn't fooled him, not for
a minute. All those tender, mushy places were
experiencing liquid fusion, and she knew it was
written all over her face. She stood to leave, busily
drying her hands on a fluffy pink bath towel.

"Yes."

"What?" she asked, confused. Then her blush
shot up two degrees. She had asked him a question and he was answering, but for the life of her
she couldn't remember the question.

"Yes, I'm hungry, but don't go to any trouble.
And, Chantal?"

"Yes?" Her voice was a weak whisper, and she
stopped her retreat toward the door, forcing herself to meet his eyes one more time.

"Thank you. You probably saved my life."

"That makes us even," she replied uneasily, not
at all sure she liked the train of his thoughts.

Jaz shook his head. "No, I still owe you one."
Not even a hint of a smile graced his mouth or lit
his eyes.

She definitely didn't like the train of his thoughts.
The last thing she needed was for Jaz Peterson to
be in her debt. Debts had a funny way of changing
the course of a person's life, and she didn't want
the responsibility for his life. She'd helped him
because she'd had to, and to relieve some of her
own debts, not to generate another obligation.
Fate wasn't as easily dismissed, and she prayed
her instincts were wrong concerning the unfore-
seen twists and turns this night had taken.

Or was the prayer something else? Her gaze lingered on a stranger's face, and she saw a myriad of other possibilities shining in his eyes. But long ago she'd learned her lesson about fate.

"You don't owe me anything, Jaz. Remember that." She stepped out of the bathroom and closed the door behind her, adding another note of finality to her statement.

Standing in front of her open refrigerator, she checked out her leftovers: mashed potatoes and gravy, fried chicken, peas, a dab of stuffing. She put a lot of everything on a plate and covered it with plastic wrap for a zap in the microwave. On second thought, she lifted the wrap and added another helping of potatoes. Plenty of carbohydrates to keep him warm all night long. She wished she'd bought an electric blanket the last time she'd been in Denver. They wanted a fortune for them in Aspen, and Elise never gave practical gifts.

She closed the refrigerator door and rested her forehead against the cool metal. What had she done? A hot, very hot, piece of jewelry was stashed in her hope chest, only a small part of her father's salvation, yet a big part of her love. What was she doing? A practically naked stranger, with a kiss that could melt the snow off the Burn, was soaking in her tub. A sheaf of stolen documents, which she hadn't even looked at, was concealed with the necklace. She needed some answers.

Rolling her head sideways, she glanced at the cedar chest where she had hidden her pack. None of your business, her conscience told her. You're already in this thing up to your neck, her curiosity replied.

Picking up her brandy in one hand and tucking a few of the many straying tendrils of hair behind her ear with the other, she crossed to the chest.

He had given her the papers, hadn't he? she thought, kneeling in front of the chest. Under duress, and to deliver, not rummage through, her conscience answered. She stared at the lock, long and hard. Then she reached.

With her eyes closed she worked the combination lock, feeling for tension in the tumblers. It was an easy trick with a cheap lock, but it kept her in practice. She should have stopped playing these childhood games a long time ago. Then the option to steal back the necklace wouldn't have been open to her.

The lock released and she opened her eyes. Regrets usually came fast on the heels of *should have*'s, and she was still too deep in the middle of this to contemplate regrets. She pulled his documents out of her pack and laid them in her lap. The words TOP SECRET stamped in red on the cover page gave her a moment's pause.

Despite her curiosity, she had no business looking at the papers he had stolen, even if they could supply her with some answers. But then again, maybe some answers were worth the risk. Come what might, a stranger was in her tub and she had promised him refuge for the night. She had a right to check him out, and the only means at her disposal were the papers. It was wonderful how the mind could work, she thought, and flipped the cover page over.

One thing became immediately clear: They were government documents, or, rather, Air Force documents. The names and ranks at the top of the page also told her they must be very important. Chantal was proud of her American citizenship, and she made a point of following the news. She had seen some of those names in the newspapers.

Fighting the temptation to look further, she closed the papers. Sandhurst could only have gotten the documents through illegal means—the same way he'd gotten her father's necklace. As best she could tell, Jaz Peterson was who he said he was, a sanctioned envoy of the American government. The thought eased her mind about the night still ahead. Then, with a twinge of regret, she realized his apparent legitimacy only widened the gulf between them.

"So what?" she whispered in self-defense, unaware that she'd voiced the words. She didn't have to live with Jaz Peterson and whatever he might think about her. She only had to live with herself.

"Dammit." His deep voice jerked her attention to the bathroom.

Chantal jumped up, the documents crunched in her fist. Guilt spread over her face like a red mask, but Jaz wasn't looking at her—yet. Still, there was no way for her to hide the papers discreetly.

Lean and lanky, he stood in the doorway, masculinity defined in its purest sense. The dusky-pink bath towel was knotted around his slim hips, hanging to his knees and showing off his dark tan to perfection. A smear of white antibiotic cream streaked across his cheek. Another trailed across the cut on his shoulder.

"Could you give me a hand with this?" he asked between his teeth, which were clamped down on a length of first-aid tape. The gauze bandage was crumpled in his hand. Then he glanced up and saw her holding the papers. His eyes narrowed as his gaze traveled from the documents to her face. He took a step forward, removing the first-aid tape from his mouth.

Seconds stretched into eternity as their eyes met, guilty blue and questioning gray.

"That's dangerous information, Chantal," he said softly. "You'd be better off not knowing."

"I didn't read them." By some miracle she kept her voice steady, despite the heat in her cheeks and the evidence in her hand. Her pride refused to allow her to give him more of an explanation. He'd either believe her or damn her, no matter how fast she talked.

"Checking me out?" he asked, lifting both dark brows.

She nodded, and Jaz thought of how deceiving looks could be. If this were their first meeting he would have thought the lady with the wild blond curls and crystalline blue eyes incapable of subterfuge, but he'd seen her in action. Regardless, he knew beyond doubt that she wasn't an arms dealer, or a thief, or a liar. General Moore might disagree with his gut instincts, but they'd gotten Jaz through more than one tight spot.

In the bathroom he had said he owed her one, and he was going to give it to her now. "That's good enough for me."

Standing in front of him and waiting, Chantal had been ready for a lot of things, but blanket acceptance hadn't been one of them. That was it? she wondered, astonished. Good enough for him?

"That's it?" she said aloud, her brow furrowed in disbelief.

"Yep, that's it. Do you think you could patch me up now?" He turned and ambled toward the fireplace, his fingers dabbing at the antibiotic cream on his shoulder. "I know you're supposed to let the air get to the wound and all that stuff, but I still think we should put a little gauze on this thing or I'll be bleeding all over your furniture."

That's it? She mouthed the words at his back as she returned the papers to the hope chest. Didn't he know those were top-secret documents she'd been looking at? Of course he knew—he was the one who'd stolen them. Strangely enough, his cavalier attitude made her mad. America deserved better protection than this. What if she had been a spy, or something?

With caution lightening every step, she followed him to where he'd dropped cross-legged on her Chinese rug. She stared down at him, but he was either oblivious of her watchful gaze or deliberately ignoring her.

"The safety of the free world's at stake and all you ask is one lousy question?" she blurted out. He nodded, and she shifted her hands lower on her hips. "You sure as hell don't make much of an interrogator, do you?"

He glanced up from inspecting his shoulder, his face the picture of calm despite her insult. "And you don't make much of a liar."

"I'm a thief, for crying out loud!" The words were out before she had time to think. Oh, brother.

"If you are, you're a damn good one. I was there, remember?"

"Remember? How could I forget?" Her voice rose to a strained pitch. "If it hadn't been for you, none of this would have happened."

"Ah-hah! Now we're getting somewhere." He scooted around to face her, a gleam of victory lighting his eyes. "I wondered when you'd get to that. But don't worry. I've got a plan to make amends."

She shot him a suspicious look. "What amends?"

"Amends for the trouble I've caused you. Whether you know it or not, we're in this thing pretty deep now. And while I've got a good cover and a great escape plan, your . . . uh, derriere is hanging out over a limb."

Her gaze narrowed another fraction of an inch. "What plan?"

Jaz had done a lot of thinking in the bathtub—it was a great place for thinking—but the look in her eye told him to keep his thoughts to himself for a while longer. "How about if we talk about it over dinner? I'm starved."

Chantal's eyes became two slits of cerulean suspicion. Jaz Peterson warmed up was proving to be as unpredictable as Jaz Peterson freezing to death in her arms. But fate could only be allowed so much rein, and it had fooled around with her long enough.

Four

She'd bandaged his shoulder while he ate. A little
poking around, by both of them, had revealed a
couple of glass chunks and no shot. He'd been a
strangely detached helper, commenting on the in-
jury and eating fried chicken as if he got blasted
off cliffs every day. Even beaten, bandaged, and
exhausted he radiated health, his body whipcord-
lean and strong, his eyes sparkling and clear. He
didn't have the pumped-up look of a weight lifter.
Rather, his muscles were well defined without
excess bulk, and Chantal was having a hard time
keeping her eyes to herself and not wondering
how it would feel to have the power of his arms
around her in passion.

The fire was dying down and the embers were
sending a soft glow over the hearth, wrapping
them in a blanket of warmth, keeping out the
cold of the night. Both of their brandy snifters
were on the polished oak floor, next to the rug
where they sat. A very cozy scene for two lovers,
Chantal thought, and for a long moment, as she
watched the last flames dance a pattern of light
over his tawny arms, she wished that they were

lovers. That there was more than one night. That he belonged to her, this stranger from fate with the clear gray eyes and easy smile.

Crazy thoughts for a crazy night.

"You really shouldn't drink anymore," she said when he reached for the brandy bottle. "Alcohol lowers your body temperature."

"I'm trying to deaden the pain." He winked, and grinned that devastating grin she was becoming all too fond of. "Don't worry, Chantal. I'm plenty warm, but I know a place where we'd be warmer." He leaned over and filled her glass. The move pulled the pink bath towel tight across his lap and exposed a generous length of one muscular tanned thigh.

Good grief, she thought, afraid for a second that the whole thing was going to fall off. When he shifted around to face her, she was sure of it. Her eyes widened and flashed to his face, but he either missed her concern or chose to ignore it, because he did nothing to secure the knot at his waist.

"Mexico. The beach at Cozumel," he continued, resting his elbows on his knees and linking his fingers over his lap. She followed every ripple of muscle down his arm. Her gaze detoured at his knee and went back up his thigh.

"I'm sure Mexico is nice and warm," she replied absently, thoroughly distracted from the conversation. The breathless quality of her voice brought her up sharp, and she forced her eyes back to his face. An equally distracting view, she realized too late. She compensated with a no-nonsense tone, asking, "Do you want to tell me what you're talking about?"

"Mexico. You, me, blue water, golden sand, a bikini. Ancient ruins, tequila." His voice softened. "Long days and longer nights."

"A bikini?" She deliberately avoided the "longer nights," easily imagining just how long those nights could get.

"For you. I'm not shy."

"No kidding." She shook her head incredulously, his plan finally becoming clear. "And I'm not going."

"A professional thief would jump at the chance for a little government interference," he informed her quietly, looking up from under spiky black lashes.

Chantal leveled her gaze on him, measuring her words carefully before she spoke. "I'm not a professional thief." Heartbeats passed, and she waited for the silence to end.

"You're too damn good to be an amateur."

Bingo. She'd had enough. With a weary sigh she rubbed her hand over her face and looked at him over the tops of her fingers. "Are you ready to go to bed yet?"

"You bet." He flashed her another one of those smiles that lit up his whole face and crinkled his eyes.

She'd walked right into that one, she silently conceded. How did he do it? Twist her around and muddle her brain? He moved faster than lightning, a speed she'd operated at more than once tonight, but he was certainly getting the best of her now.

She cleared her throat with a small sound and said, "I'll make this as simple as possible. You, bed." She pointed at him, then back at herself. "Me, couch."

"Okay." He half shrugged a reluctant acceptance with his right shoulder, but his come-on smile held firm. "Now, what about Mexico?"

"I'm not running," she said, pushing up off the rug. She didn't get two inches before his hand covered her leg and held her to the floor.

"Then don't run away from me, Chantal. I may be the only chance you've got." His voice was grim, his smile fading into a worried line and his eyes darkening with concern. Powerful fingers curled halfway around her slender thigh, holding her with gentle strength—gentle, but unbreakable.

Chantal didn't even try to release herself, the truth of what he said holding her more firmly than his hand. She knew exactly what he meant. They had left a mess from the library to her front door, and she wasn't sure what to do about it. Her gaze drifted to the fire, and she watched the ebbing flames flicker and die, then flicker again as they raced along the edges of the coals.

"You're in trouble, big trouble." He voiced her thoughts perfectly. "How long do you think it's going to take Sandhurst to pick up our trail? A week? A couple of days? Try tomorrow morning. And it's not going to be me he finds, Chantal. It's going to be you—unless you come with me. I can offer you the same protection the government is giving me."

"Are you some kind of spy?" Damn, she wished she had looked at those papers.

"No." His soft chuckle eased the seriousness back out of the mood. "I'm strictly free-lance. Doing a favor for a friend."

"Free-lance what?" Questioning him was a lot better than having him dig around in her murky past.

"Private detective. I've got a business, if you can call it that, in Cozumel. Tracker of wayward wives and objects of dubious value, that's me."

Pure skepticism twisted the corners of her mouth and narrowed her gaze. "Since when does the government pull in a PI to do its dirty work?"

"Since whenever it has its claws in one and needs somebody expendable," he said offhandedly. "I used to be one of the country's finest."

"You must have screwed up real bad," she said bluntly.

"Let's just say I was in the wrong place at the wrong time and on the wrong end of the totem pole." That's right, Jaz, he thought, win her over with the unvarnished truth. Two years had made the screw-up easier to live with, but only to a point—which didn't include broadcasting his mistake to all comers. On the other hand, that disaster had led him into this one, led him into this night and to this woman. If he got on his afternoon flight the next day, he'd be in Cozumel before the sun set, and sure as hell he'd be setting himself up for a bout of sleepless nights haunted by exotic blue eyes and a golden mane of silky hair. He couldn't desert her. His responsibility for her precarious position was one reason. The woman herself was a bigger one. She triggered feelings he'd been out of touch with for a long, long time, and he was thoroughly intrigued, with her and with his response.

So he had a few secrets of his own, Chantal thought. Let him keep his and she could keep hers. No more should be asked of strangers.

She redirected the conversation. "What about the police?"

"Jimmy might have called them in on your trick, but he sure as hell isn't going to call them in on mine." A thoughtful look crossed his face. "In a way I guess you could say I did you a big favor by bumping into you." She gave him a look that told him in no uncertain terms he was stretching his luck.

"Okay," he conceded. "Maybe not a favor, but I can do one for you now."

"Why?" she asked. It would be so easy for him to walk away.

Good question, Jaz thought. Damn good question. His gaze wandered from her bare feet and the pearlescent polish on her toes, to the damp blond waves curling over her lavender corduroy shirt. So many contradictions in such a small package.

She was tough enough to pull off a complicated heist without a flicker of hesitation, step by step, with a mind like a steel trap. She hadn't even flinched when he'd walked in on her. She had sized him up with a burning concentration he'd felt all the way across the library and then she'd taken care of business.

Soft enough to care when he'd needed her, and even softer each time he'd kissed her. Her full lower lip had trembled beneath his, her tongue teasing the inside of his mouth and driving him just a little bit wild. Sweetness, passion, and intelligence. He doubted if he'd ever be the same after spending the night with this woman named Chantal Cochard.

But the wariness in her azure eyes warned him that he couldn't tell her those things, so he opted for the strictly logical.

"Because you deserve my help," he said. "I wouldn't have made it without you—not on the roof, not on the mountain . . . and not in the bathtub." A hint of a grin once again teased the corner of his mouth, deepening the crease in one lean cheek.

She blushed at the memory and lowered her gaze. "I won't run, Jaz. I can't run."

"Can you hide?"

She glanced up. "That bad?"

"That bad, Chantal." He reached out and cupped her chin in his palm, barely resisting the urge to draw her close and taste her mouth again. "Sandhurst is going to tear this town upside down and inside out looking for what I took from him, and he's going to start on that hot trail we left. I was careful—he won't track us to your cabin—but people like you usually have a reputation, and he's got a lot of connections. Does he know who you are?"

"Know me?" she blurted out. "That crook tried to steal my commission!"

His face became very still, his voice very soft. "What kind of commission?"

"Real estate," she informed him, and Jaz felt his heart sink. "If it hadn't been for Elise, he might have gotten away with it, too. But she's a barracuda."

"Who is Elise?" He was almost afraid to ask.

"My aunt, and my broker."

"Great." He moaned, dropping his head into his hands. "I suppose Sandhurst knows it's your necklace, too." His lady was going down fast. *His lady?*

"Of course not," she snapped, her voice edged with irritation. "Besides, it's not my necklace."

"Do you want to explain that?" An aching pulse was starting to beat under the fingers pressed to his temples, a sure sign the night was catching up to him.

"It belongs to my father. It was stolen from his jewelry store."

The pulse eased off, and Jaz opened his eyes and stared at the shadows in his palms. "Is he the one who taught you?" In his whole career, public and private, it was one of the longest connections he'd ever made, but he had a feeling, a strong feeling. Jewelry dealer—jewelry thief. Maybe the connection wasn't so long.

"You're better at the interrogation game than I thought," she said slowly. "True confessions is over for the night, Jaz."

And just when he was getting his second wind. Damn.

"Okay, Chantal. We'll let your mysterious past ride for the night. We've got more important things to talk about—like the sleeping arrangements," he said hopefully. The look she gave him dashed the last of his aspirations on that front. "How about Mexico? My flight doesn't leave until two o'clock."

Three things roused Jaz from slumber: a knock on the door, a muffled noise—which sounded suspiciously like a five-foot, two-inch body falling off a red velvet sofa—and the accompanying cry of dismay.

They had argued until dawn, with him on the losing end most of the night. The only fight he hadn't minded losing was the one about who got the bed. Actually, he had minded. He'd thought the queen-sized mattress was big enough for both of them. She had begged to differ, and now she'd fallen off the couch. She should have slept with him.

"Are you okay?" he mumbled into the pillow, not quite bothering to wake up. The pillows were limp and abundant, just the way he liked them, and all of the bed linen smelled softly of Chantal. Lace-edged flannel sheets scented with her fragrance had woven her image through the shadows of sleep, making reality the less-pleasant option of the moment. He chose to continue his dreams and let his mind drift backward to the place where Chantal touched him with passion and whispered in his ear. A groan sighed from his lips.

"Yes . . . no . . . Jaz, get up!"

Part of his consciousness heard her struggling with her blankets, resented the intrusion, and figured she could handle them alone. He snuggled more deeply under his with an answering grunt.

Mornings weren't his best time. Half a bottle of brandy, very little sleep, and a body that felt like his rented Jeep weren't making this one any exception, unless he was allowed to dream. She should have slept with him, he thought again. This was as harmless as he got.

"I mean it! Get up!" The blankets came whooshing off his body in the rudest of awakenings and just as quickly came whooshing back. "Good Lord! You're naked!"

Jaz gave up. He grinned a sleepy grin and rolled over onto his back, discreetly covered by his once-warm, now-cool blankets. "That's what I love about you, Chantal," he said lazily. "Your keen eye for detail."

She pinned him with a steely glare and jerked the blankets to the foot of the bed again. Her eyes didn't flicker from his, not once. "Get into that bathroom, and don't you dare come out," she ordered.

He broadened his grin and reached for the pink towel he'd left on the bed. "Irate boyfriend?" he asked, nodding toward the door and the persistent knocks emanating from the other side. The seductive woman of his dreams was a spitting kitten in real life, a very rumpled kitten. One of her suspenders hung around her hip, her lavender shirt was only half tucked into her jeans, and her hair was wild, really wild, every silver-gold strand finding its own unique direction.

"I don't have a boyfriend. Now, will you—" She broke off, a simultaneous thought crossing both their minds.

"Sandhurst!"

Jaz jumped off the bed, almost killing himself with the effort. But he was awake. Man, was he awake.

Chantal slammed her fist into the bedpost and

shook her head with disgust. Lord, what a pair they made.

"Don't panic." He grabbed her arms, the towel dangling uselessly from one hand. *Give me strength,* she prayed, keeping her eyes focused on his. "Play it easy. I swear to God, unless he's a bloodhound he didn't track me all the way here." Laying the false leads was what had almost done him in the night before.

"I promise," she said through clenched teeth, "I won't panic. Now, will you just get yourself decent and go in the bathroom?"

An instant twinkle lit the gray depths of his eyes. "I don't know, babe," he drawled, a wicked grin teasing his mouth. "Is that a little panic I feel coming off of you?"

"Jaz." She drew his name out in warning.

He dropped a quick kiss on the top of her head and, bare buns flexing, sauntered across the room. Chantal waited for the morning matinee to end before heading toward the door. Criminy, she thought, even his butt was tan.

The bathroom was huge, considering the size of the rest of the cabin, and in daylight Jaz noticed the walls weren't white, but pale pink, a romantic contrast to the black claw-footed bathtub. The shutters were open on the frosty, small-paned window above the white pedestal sink. He smiled at the unusual placement, silently agreeing that he'd rather look at a mountain meadow than his own face first thing in the morning. A large wood-framed mirror hung on the wall above an antique vanity table and bench.

Jaz had no sooner noted the layout and closed the bathroom door, when he heard the front door open.

"Good morning, Mrs. Palmer. What has you up and about this morning?" Lord, she had a sweet voice, Jaz thought, relaxing his bruised body against the door. And she was pouring sugar into it for Mrs. Palmer, the wonderful Mrs. Palmer.

"Hardly morning, dear. It's almost noon."

Jaz checked his watch, a grimace passing over his face. "Damn," he muttered. Two hours until flight time.

"Josh sent me over to check on you," Mrs. Palmer continued, "what with all the excitement last night."

Chantal ran her fingers through her hair, trying to shake the image of a naked Jaz sprawled across her bed, a naked Jaz parading around her cabin. She was struggling to concentrate on what Lily Palmer, a bundle of red parka and salt-and-pepper braids, was saying. Long, muscular legs entwined with her lace-edged sheets and stretching in a lazy stride were winning, hands down.

"Excitement?" she stammered.

"At first Josh thought our propane tank had blown. Or yours. He checked around outside, but there weren't any fires in Timbers." Timbers was the name of the area where they lived. It comprised forty one-acre lots, and the Palmers had bought the first two. They'd built their own large home on one and the small cabin they rented to Chantal on the other. Chantal held the listings on the remaining plots, thanks to Roger Neville, a real-estate developer and her aunt's answer for Chantal's happily-every-after.

". . . absolutely bounced us out of bed!"

"Explosion?" Chantal repeated weakly.

"Don't worry, dear. Josh called Sheriff Lowe early this morning." Lily patted her shoulder with a mittened hand. "He should be here any time."

Without warning, Chantal's knees buckled,

barely locking in time to keep her from hitting the floor. She would have had plenty of company. Her heart, her stomach, and her confidence had all congealed in the vicinity of her feet. Her mind raced over the night. She'd left no prints, no equipment, and no distinguishing tracks. The only clues were the rope and the snowmobile, and both belonged to Jaz.

The cherubic face of Lily Palmer crinkled in concern, the care lines and laugh lines melding into motherly solicitude. The mitten came to rest on Chantal's cheek. "You work too hard, honey. Josh noticed your lights on into the wee hours. Them little orphans aren't going to feel better by your wearing yourself to a frazzle. Did you eat the fried-chicken dinner I sent home with you the other night?"

"Yes, Mrs. Palmer," she lied. "It was delicious." No lie this time. Jaz had loved every bite.

"Such lovely, old-world manners." The mitten patted and patted her cheek. "Well, don't you worry, honey. Sheriff Lowe will get to the bottom of this."

"That's wonderful." Her words sounded as sick as she felt. Thankfully, Lily didn't seem to notice, and her mitten added one final pat to Chantal's pale face.

"Well, you drop over and see us real soon, and don't hesitate to bring your young man. Josh and I are very liberated about these things. Three grown sons don't allow you to live in the past."

"My . . . young . . . man?" The words dropped from Chantal's lips in dismay, each one softer than the one before. Her stomach started churning its way up from the floor into a knot in her middle.

"Goodness," Lily said, clucking. "I didn't mean to embarrass you. But when you didn't answer right away, I peeked through the window."

Omigod.

Lily lowered her voice to a conspiratorial whisper. "He's quite handsome, isn't he? A little on the thin side, but don't tell him that. Men are so vain. Just fatten him up. I'll copy off some recipes for you."

Chantal's hand fluttered to her breast. "Mrs. Palmer," she said with a gasp, then had to stop to catch her breath. "Mrs. Palmer, I slept on the couch." She swung her arm out behind her, in the general direction of the blanket-smothered sofa.

"Some nights are like that, honey." Lily shook her head a little sadly and opened the door. "He'll get over it," she assured the younger woman.

Chantal closed the door and leaned her head on the solid oak panel. Anyone who moved to the mountains for privacy was crazy, she thought. The fewer people per square mile, the more interested they were in each other—helpfully, curiously, dangerously interested. Lily knew everything except that the necklace and papers were in the hope chest.

It wasn't that bad, she told herself, trying to buck up her spirits.

"Your young man can't find his clothes." The husky drawl drew her attention to the bathroom. "But I used the new toothbrush I found in your cabinet."

Chantal turned around, leaning against the door for support. Her gaze flickered over the lanky body lounging against the bathroom jamb. Long after he was gone, the dusky-pink bath towel would hold memories for her. Low on his slim hips, hanging by a thread . . . Certainly she'd never worn it with such style.

Lily Palmer was wrong; he wasn't too thin. And Lily Palmer was right; he was quite handsome, his sun-streaked hair tousled by sleep and sweeping around the back of his neck, his face lean and boyish, his eyes crinkled by the teasing smile curving his mouth. A real heartbreaker. But not of her heart.

"Your clothes are in the dryer," she said. She'd laundered them during the lulls in their late-night–early-morning contest of wills. "I'd offer you a cup of coffee, but we'd better hit the road and get you out of here before the sheriff arrives."

Good-bye came closer to reality, and Chantal suddenly felt she was making the biggest mistake of her life. That feeling was getting pretty easy for her to recognize. She'd had it at least a dozen times in the last twenty-four hours. Why should it be hard to let him go? Regardless, she had to get rid of him. By her estimation, he was the biggest clue in the valley.

"Kicking me out, huh?" he asked.

" 'Fraid so, Jaz." She pushed herself away from the door and headed for the kitchen, not giving her doubts a chance to form on her face.

"Then I'm *not* going to get over your sleeping on the couch last night," he informed her with a quick wink before disappearing into the bathroom.

How did he do it? she wondered. His body was bruised, beaten, and had to hurt like hell, but he'd awakened with a smile. She hung over the sink without a smile in sight. She let the water run over her fingers, ignoring the stiffness and pain in her palms from the rope burns. When the water reached a bearable temperature, she pulled a clean dish towel off the shelf, wet one end, and buried her face into the steaming warmth. What else could possibly go wrong with her life?

A knock sounded on the door. What was this? Grand Central Station?

"Go away, Mrs. Palmer," she mumbled into the towel. She wasn't going to put her fight-or-flight system into gear again until she knew it was absolutely necessary. Her heart couldn't take it.

The knock came again, and with a heavy groan Chantal dragged herself back across the cabin to open the door.

The quintessence of dark-eyed, blond beauty waited on the other side.

Dumbfounded, Chantal had a hard time finding her voice. "Elise," she finally croaked out. "What are you doing here?"

With a practiced air of sophisticated nonchalance, Elise breezed into the room. "I was showing the Fullers the Laurance listing. It's just over the hill." She pirouetted in front of the fireplace, slipping out of her voluminous Russian sable fur. One finely arched brow lifted in question as she spotted the pile of bed linen on the couch. "Guests?" she asked coolly.

Before Chantal could get out a single word of explanation, the "guest" strode out of the bathroom.

"Chantal?" Struggling with his sweater, Jaz failed to notice the other woman watching his entrance. "You're going to have to pin this thing, or something. You really did a job . . . Hello," he greeted Elise easily. Chantal decided right then and there that she was going to leave the country and spend the rest of her days learning how to cope with embarrassment. She'd start in the bathroom, just in case she threw up during the first lesson.

"Excuse me." She smiled wanly and turned on her heel.

Slightly perplexed, Jaz watched her retreat. Something was going on, something he didn't understand. Chantal had scaled the Sandhurst mansion, faced gunfire, and held her own with him all night, but this lady had her running.

Covering his confusion, he gracefully picked up the pieces of her ignominious retreat, stepping forward and extending his hand to Elise.

"I'm Jaz Peterson. You must be Chantal's aunt." The resemblance was remarkable, he thought, but where his lady was all sweetness and light, this lady was not. She was beautiful, very beautiful. Her face was a study in artful design, natural and applied, especially applied. High-boned cheeks were blushed with copper color. Her chocolate-brown eyes were outlined with layers of careful makeup, highlighting the contrast with her bluntly cut pale gold hair and lightly tanned face. What Jaz knew about clothes could be summed up in two words— not much. But this lady was dressed to kill, in leather and gold, real gold. The yards of fur draped over her arm spoke for themselves. He'd seen that slightly jaded look in her eyes many times on the beaches of the Caribbean, women who controlled their world with wealth and enough beauty to hold back the years.

The older, more calculated version of Chantal accepted his hand, albeit lightly. "Elise Stahl." Her shadowed eyes measured him shrewdly, from his bare feet, up his wrinkled pants, to the mangled sweater falling off his bandaged shoulder.

Jaz knew without asking that he'd been found lacking. "Excuse me." His own smile felt a little wan under her canny gaze. He also felt like a fool for mimicking Chantal's retreat, but he did it anyway.

He closed the bathroom door behind him, and the first words out of his mouth were, "How long are we going to hide out in here?"

Chantal moaned. "Until I die."

She was balanced on the edge of the glossy black bathtub, her face hidden in her hands, her toes stretched to the floor.

"Okay. It's noon now. If she's not gone by nightfall, we'll make a run for it."

"Don't make me laugh."

Jaz seriously doubted he was in any danger of making her laugh. He pulled the vanity bench in front of the bathtub and sat down facing her. Sliding his arms around her waist, he rested his forehead on hers, feeling the satiny texture of her skin against his, the silkiness of her hair falling next to his face.

"Aren't you a little old to be explaining your love life?" he asked, confusion apparent in every word.

"I don't have a love life," she mumbled.

Now they were getting somewhere. "What a coincidence. Me neither. Maybe we should team up."

"Oh, Jaz." She slowly wound her arms around his neck, burrowing her face into his good shoulder. Her soft breath blew across his nape and sent a heated shiver down his spine. "What am I going to do?"

A few possibilities crossed Jaz's mind, all but one of them unmentionable in her current state of distress. Controlling some very strong instincts he said only, "Come with me."

Her fingers tunneled into his hair, and his control melted. He opened his mouth low on her neck, under the collar of her shirt, and nuzzled the tender skin there. "Come with me, Chantal," he murmured.

She gently forced his head back, her eyes luminous and sad. "I'm never going to be able to explain you." The words were whispered urgently, as if they held more importance than he could possibly imagine. Which they did.

"That wasn't the question, babe," he said dryly, a self-mocking grin twitching his mouth. She definitely wasn't with him on this latest merger attempt.

"Elise is going to expect an explanation, and I can't tell her the truth."

"Yeah, because you're a lousy liar. Why don't you comb your hair and fix your clothes and let me explain myself? I've had a lot of practice." Years of it, he thought ruefully, explaining himself to tougher numbers than the divine Ms. Stahl.

"Trust me," he continued when she looked doubtful. "I can handle this problem. Then, later, you can tell me what the problem is. Okay?" His eyebrows rose hopefully.

He was darn-near irresistible when he looked at her like that, Chantal thought. A hint of a smile curved her mouth. How was she ever going to explain Elise to Jaz, let alone Jaz to Elise? He didn't know the weak-willed, subservient Chantal, and she'd just as soon not have told him. It took her an instant to realize how strange the thought was. Jaz was leaving. She wouldn't be explaining anything to him—except a good-bye he wouldn't accept. Along came another one of those pangs of regret, tightening her heart and refusing to be ignored.

"Just keep it simple, Jaz. I'll be out in a minute." Her natural survival instincts were reasserting themselves. If she couldn't lie her way out of this faux pas, she'd try bluffing, but not without some serious preparation.

"That's the spirit," he said. "Now, about this sweater . . ."

She slipped off the bathtub and hustled up some safety pins, putting him back together with a recommendation that he wear his jacket for a more respectable look.

"I don't think she's going to be impressed by my jean jacket, even if it does have a sheepskin collar," he said wryly.

"I can guarantee it." Chantal gave his sweater

one last tug before surveying her handiwork. He looked like what he was, a refugee from disaster. "But wear it anyway."

"You got it, partner." He rose slowly from the bench, his hands trailing up either side of her body, a broad grin crinkling his eyes. "How about a little fooling around before I throw myself to the lions? Might be your last chance," he warned in a low, teasing voice.

Once again, without any bidding, the image of Jaz lying on her bed returned. Chantal swallowed hard and very gently unpried his fingers from her hips. The man was incorrigible. The man was too much. The man was getting to her. The sooner she got rid of him the better . . . and the worse.

"Just keep it simple," she advised lightly, keeping her incomprehensible sadness to herself.

She'd no sooner gotten his hands off her body when they cupped her face. Incorrigible.

"They have a word for that, Chantal." He tilted her head back, and she found herself gazing into river-clear eyes.

"Word?"

"Kiss," he drawled. "Keep It Simple Stupid." His mouth turned up at one corner, and he lowered his head to hers.

"I never said stu—" The word disappeared as his lips claimed hers, softly, tenderly, then much too quickly released her.

Chantal didn't watch him leave. Her eyes had drifted closed with the returning pleasure of his touch, but unfortunately she couldn't help but overhear his opening statement.

"Chantal will be out in a minute. She's just getting off to a rough start this morning. We had a . . . long night." His tone hinted at more than the length of the night, and without actually seeing him she knew exactly which smile he was turning on Elise—the half-crooked, half-teasing one that usually came with a quick lift of his eyebrows. She was going to throttle him.

But first she had to throw herself together. Rummaging through her vanity drawer, she grabbed blushes, shadows, and glosses. She snapped up a long, curved barrette and stuck it in her mouth, using her hands to twist and curl her hair on top of her head in a softly messy Gibson. The barrette went in one side and a number of bobby pins went in all around. She brushed her teeth and stripped off her clothes at the same time, spitting out toothpaste while she shimmied out of her jeans.

A slip slid down her body and a pair of hose slid up. Her fingers flipped through the hangers in the closet until she found the perfect outfit, a mid-calf white angora sheath with a cowl neck.

"Damn," she muttered. She should have done her hair last.

Carefully she eased the dress over her head, then smoothed it over her hips. A pair of slant-heeled chamois boots added the inches she needed to carry off the length. She cinched a matching chamois belt with a silver cowboy buckle around her waist, tucking the belt end under the side.

Two smears of mauve eye shadow, eight or nine strokes of mascara, and a dusting of blush later, she was almost ready to go. She dipped her finger into the gloss pot and rubbed it over her lips. For the final touch she chose silver jewelry, a squash-blossom necklace and a pair of sterling feathers that swept up around her ears rather than dangled.

Now all she needed was a deep breath, which she took, and an ounce of courage, which she found. Steeling herself for the worst, she opened the door and marched into the fray.

But there was no fray. The bed had been made,

the blankets from the couch were neatly folded at
its foot, and the aroma of fresh-brewed coffee com-
peted with the pine scent coming from the crack-
ling fire. Chantal knew her aunt hadn't accom-
plished any of this; Elise hadn't made a bed in
twenty years. She shot a confused glance at Jaz,
expecting a self-satisfied grin and maybe a teasing wink. That was not what she found.

He stood at the edge of the kitchen, a slightly
dazed look softening the lean angles of his face
and clouding the shaded gray depths of his eyes.
Her confusion melted into bewitchment under the
lingering track of his gaze as it roamed over her
body. Curve by curve she felt him burn her image
into a private place in his mind. Then his eyes
met hers, capturing them with a promise, and
she knew it was more than her image this stranger
was stealing. It was her heart. Second after pulsing second he was stealing her heart into . . .

Forever, Jaz thought. That was where he would
take her, into forever. Every fantasy he'd ever had
was standing in the middle of the room, and she
belonged to him. He'd wanted the pixie burglar
with the mystery face and soft mouth. He'd de-
sired the partner who'd saved his life and held
him close. But this woman, the elfin princess
with the tumbledown hair and silver amulets, she
belonged to him. She was the woman he would
bury himself in, lose himself in, and die for time
after time. A thousand nights of dreams had promised him so.

Five

"Roger called this morning," Elise said frostily, shattering the trancelike spell. "He has invited us to dinner at the Hotel."

Chantal dragged her eyes away from Jaz to stare at her aunt. Her heart was pounding so heavily and slowly, it took her a moment to respond. "What?" she asked.

"Roger has invited us to dinner tonight at the Hotel," Elise repeated, more than a hint of irritation clipping her words. She was perched on the edge of the wing chair, her legs crossed and one foot tapping a staccato beat on the floor.

Chantal let the words sink in, all the way to the seemingly ever-present knot in her stomach. At least the morning was staying in one groove, disaster from beginning to end, she thought. There was only one capital-*H* hotel in Aspen, the Hotel Orleans, which was practically a private salon for the Sandhursts. And there was only one Roger in Chantal's life. Roger Neville, ten years her senior and definitely not too thin. Rich and in real-estate development, he was everything Elise had ever looked for in a man—for her niece.

"How lovely." What her voice lacked in enthusiasm Chantal tried to make up for by plastering a feeble smile to her face.

"Dinner is at eight, cocktails at seven-thirty," Elise informed her without a hint of a thaw in her voice. Considering that Jaz was only ten feet away, Elise was doing a marvelous job of pretending he wasn't there, Chantal thought.

"Yes, well . . ." she stammered, her senses tangling with her own awareness of the man standing in her kitchen. "I'll meet you at the Hotel. I have a few errands to run this afternoon."

Throwing caution to the wind, she shot a quick glance at her errand. Unlike her, he appeared totally at ease, fully recovered from the out-of-nowhere magic. He was wearing his jean jacket, lounging with his hip against the counter, drinking his coffee. His ankles were crossed, and one hand was shoved deep into the front pocket of his black slacks. But he was still watching her, every breath she took, and a definite gleam of challenge had lit the depths of his eyes.

She turned back to Elise. She wasn't ready for that kind of challenge, not this morning, not when all he had to do was look at her and she lost track of reality.

"Can I freshen your coffee?" She took a hesitant step toward her aunt.

"No, thank you. I think I'll let you run your errands"—she flicked a desultory glance over Jaz, as only she could—"and I'll see you at dinner tonight. Don't be late. You know how Roger dislikes tardiness."

"Yes, I know." Mentally Chantal added to Roger's list of dislikes undeveloped land just sitting there doing nothing except looking good, developed land that didn't turn a profit, and empty condo units during the height of the season. Roger had a one-track mind, business. But he was congenial, very taken with her, and marginally less manipulative than Elise. Chantal was a sucker for emotional blackmail, and Elise had it down to a fine art. Chantal's biggest rebellion in ten years had been moving into the cabin.

In her more reflective moments Chantal realized the guilt from Monaco spilled over into her relationship with her aunt, but the realization didn't lessen her sense of obligation. Elise had accepted her and taught her how to make a place for herself in the world apart from her past. Chantal enjoyed selling real estate and she enjoyed knowing how to look her best, one of the first things Elise had taught her. Growing up in a family of men hadn't lent itself to makeup sessions and shopping sprees.

She did not enjoy Roger as anything more than a friend, and that situation had been coming to a head long before Jaz Peterson had stepped into her life, kissing her to distraction and invading her thoughts.

"Let me help you with your coat," she offered quickly when Elise rose from the chair, but before she rounded the sofa, Jaz was there, sweeping the older woman into the full-length fur.

Finally Elise had to acknowledge him. "Mr. Peterson." The thank you was barely implied and definitely not said.

Chantal felt more than a little embarrassment for her aunt's unusual but effective rudeness. He must have had a rough time out here alone, she thought. He didn't look any the worse for wear, but her heart went out to him anyway—the way it had been doing ever since he'd kissed her on the roof. Had it only been the night before?

"My pleasure, Ms. Stahl."

Chantal caught his wink out of the corner of her eye. You're wasting your charm, Jaz, she told him silently. But then, you've got plenty of it to waste, don't you? His grin told her he was reading her like a book, but anything was better than— and nothing was as good as—having him melt her with those eyes.

Heels clicking on the hardwood floor, Elise walked to door and swung it open. Then, just as quickly, without leaving, she swung it closed.

"Chantal, dear?" Her voice wavered in an uncharacteristic tremor, and Chantal was immediately alert.

"Yes, Elise?" she asked carefully, wishing Elise would leave so she could start putting her life back into a semblance of order.

"Is there anything you need before I leave?" Elise hesitated, turning a worried gaze back on her niece. "Like an alibi?"

The words dropped into a breathless silence, which was instantly broken by Jaz and Chantal stumbling over each other in their haste to get to the window.

"Ouch!"

"Damn!"

"Oh, my God!"

"Don't panic." Jaz swung her away from the window. "He's looking for propane tanks, not us. Remember that."

Elise paled to an unflattering shade of ash white, but she didn't faint. By the time the knock sounded on the door, she had pulled herself together, Chantal had pulled herself together, and Jaz had pulled himself and Chantal together, with his hurt arm draped around her shoulders.

The awkward trio of two nervous women and

one too-calm man greeted the sheriff when Elise opened the door.

Big and burly, Sheriff Lowe stood on the threshold, ramrod-straight, his uniform pressed to within an inch of its life. His eyes were hidden by a pair of aviator sunglasses, reflecting three pairs of wary eyes in turn. A heavy black holster holding a .357 was slung around his waist.

"Good afternoon, Ms. Stahl." He tipped his hat. "I didn't expect to run into you way out here in the sticks."

"Hello, Sheriff Lowe. You know my niece, Chantal Cochard." Elise gestured at her niece, her tone and action hitting all the grace notes, right on target. Of all of them in the room, only Chantal knew Elise well enough to detect the edge of panic in her dark eyes. "I believe you met at the charity fund-raiser we hosted last year."

"Ms. Cochard." He tipped his hat again. "Will Lodestar Realty be putting on another charity ball this year? Your last one sure was successful. Of course, in a town of deep pockets we ought to be able to come up with something for those less fortunate."

"Yes, yes, we should," Chantal agreed shakily, her chin tilted up to meet her reflection in the glasses. Jaz's fingers tightened on her shoulder, and she forced her mouth into a tremulous smile. "And we did. We raised over fifty thousand in that one night. Please come in, Sheriff Lowe. No sense in heating the whole outdoors."

"Thank you, ma'am." He stepped in and Elise closed the door, flashing her a cautious look from behind his back.

"Lily Palmer came over this morning and told me she had called you," Chantal continued, cringing inwardly, wondering what Elise was imagining.

Or worse, guessing. "I don't know what I can tell you. We heard the explosion, too, but nothing else." She emphasized the *we* and glanced up at Jaz, giving him what she hoped was an adoring look. He grinned and linked his other arm over her breasts, clasping his hands just below her shoulder.

"Well, ma'am. We found the explosion a couple of miles from here, up in the Forest Service land. It was a snowmobile. We haven't had any reports of a missing vehicle, but somebody was up there, and up to something. A lot of strange things were going on all over this mountain last night," he added, seemingly to himself, but it was hard to tell through the glasses. "I'd appreciate it if you'd keep your eyes open and call me if you see anything."

Jaz had been right, Chantal thought, wiping one avenue of disaster off her list. Sandhurst must have called off the alarm.

"Of course, Sheriff," she said somewhat more smoothly, hating the way her life was filling up with lies. She made a move to extend her hand, but Jaz captured it with his and squeezed lightly. The instant stab of pain reminded her of what she never should have forgotten—her palms were a mess from rappelling down the mansion and cliff. "We'll call if we notice anything." She snuggled closer under Jaz's arm and wrapped her arms around his waist under his jacket. His body was warm and hard beneath her fingers, and she wondered how long it would take her to forget how he felt, wondered how long she'd want to remember. Two peas in a pod, two bugs in the same cocoon, they stuck together like glue.

Elise picked up on the not-so-subtle exchange and extended her own hand to the sheriff. "I'll be calling you real soon, Sheriff," she crooned, completely back in control. "The Lodestar Charity Ball is coming up in a couple of months, and we'll want you and your lovely wife, Debbie, there."

"Thank you, ma'am. We sure had a good time last year." He shook her hand, tipped his hat, and left with another round of *thank you*'s.

Chantal sent her own silent thank you to heaven for Elise's well-planned guest list and her incredible memory. She couldn't have come up with "Debbie" to save her life.

Elise turned back around from waving the sheriff off the porch.

"Chantal, I think"—her glance took in the two of them, still wrapped together like braided rope—"I think we should have lunch tomorrow. Yes, definitely lunch." She pulled the fur collar tightly around her neck and bestowed a look of dark suspicion on Jaz. Then she turned to Chantal, and the look lightened only a few shades. "Don't forget about dinner with Roger tonight." It was a command, not a reminder. She swept out of the cabin.

Chantal sagged against Jaz's body. Lunch. One of those lunches. She knew the time and the place without Elise's telling her. *Oh, brother.*

"We make a helluva team, lady."

"You got that right," she mumbled into his sweater. "Ever since we met, everything's been going straight to—"

"Heaven," he interrupted in a husky whisper, cupping her face in his hands.

His calloused fingers were rough against her skin, rough and infinitely gentle, as he tilted her head back. All night long she had wondered what she'd do if he kissed her again, and now she knew. Twice she had melted in his arms; this time would be no different. *Just one last kiss before good-bye.*

They were finally alone, and Jaz had waited long enough for another taste of forever. He meant to kiss her, to draw her deep inside him with his mouth, until all she felt was him—and he knew she knew it. Sooty lashes lowered over smoky-blue eyes. Anticipation softened her mouth and tightened his gut, hurting and feeling good at the same time.

He lowered his mouth, skimming his tongue across her lips and rubbing his nose down the side of hers, teasing, telegraphing his need without taking what he needed—her kiss, her mouth moving over his, her hands touching him.

"Kiss me, Chantal." He blew the words on her lips, holding her a breath away, waiting for the response he already felt pulsing under the tender skin beneath his fingers. When it came, when she lifted her lips to his, he sealed their mouths and plundered slowly, savoring each portion of sweetness she gave, letting her lead him deeper into the magic. But each moment of enchantment demanded another, until he wanted more than a kiss.

His hand slid to the small of her back and lower, pressing her into the cradle of his hips, needing her that close and closer. The soft angora clung to her curves and hid nothing from his exploring hand, not the tautness of her buttocks and thighs, not the quivering response of her body. With just her kiss, with just the erotic forays of her tongue into his mouth, his body began the inexorable tightening toward a higher pleasure. Sinew by sinew, a smoldering heat spread toward his groin. He slowly rubbed his hand up under her arm to her breast and rolled his lower body against hers, igniting the flame only she could quench, catching her gasps of pleasure with his mouth and still wanting more.

Chantal was drowning in his seduction, and dying for what she couldn't have. Heavy waves of pleasure weakened her knees as his kiss weakened her will, hinting at the sensual delights he offered. His other kisses hadn't prepared her for the depth of feeling he was capable of evoking. Nothing had. She turned her mouth deeper into his, loath to let him go, and ran her hands under his sweater, needing to feel him once more—the soft heat of his skin, the tightness of his muscles—for the long nights ahead when the memories of a stranger would haunt her. His response was immediate and undeniable, his body hardening against all her softest places.

He angled his mouth away from hers and laid a trail of wet, biting kisses to her neck. "Make love with me, Chantal." His voice ached with the same need sweeping through her body. His tongue traced and licked the delicate contours of her ear. His teeth grazed the peach-sweet skin of her nape. "Make love with me."

She was going to hate herself, already hated herself, for the answer on her lips. Fate should have known better than to set her up with a one-night stand. Tearing herself from him, she took a step away, needing a clean break.

"Jaz, I'm taking you back," she whispered sadly. "Back to where you were supposed to be last night." Her hand tightened in a fist on her abdomen. How had he come to mean so much? Even breathing hurt. Eyes filled with all the regret in her heart pleaded with him to understand.

But he didn't understand. He looked as if somebody had kicked him in the gut, his face stark and vulnerable with the passion he needed to share. He stepped forward, his hand reaching.

"No," she whispered, shaking her head. She

couldn't make love and watch him go. And she couldn't go with him, wouldn't run again.

Desire-darkened eyes held hers across the emptiness, and the light of passion was slowly extinguished behind a veil of frustration. A muscle twitched along his tightly clenched jaw. "This doesn't settle anything, Chantal," he said roughly. Nothing could hide the harsh edge of disappointment in his voice.

No, he didn't understand, she thought, but better his anger than his pain. She retrieved the documents from her chest and handed them to him, then turned on her heel and crossed the cabin to her armoire.

Shrugging into a calf-length coyote coat, another expensive present from Elise, she said, "I'll meet you in the car." Then, without another glance, she strode past him and out the door.

The ride to Jaz's hotel was made in silence. There was nothing left to say. He'd told her Snowmass Village, and she made all the turns by instinct, onto Highway 82, the left turn up Brush Creek. She pulled her blue economy car to a stop under the canopy of the StoneTree Lodge. Elise hadn't come through with a sports car; she was waiting for Roger to do that.

Chantal kept the car in gear, the engine idling. No more regrets, she promised herself even as her throat tightened.

"I'm going to need some help. Set the brake and throw her in neutral," he commanded softly.

What did he think—that this was easy for her? She jerked the shift into neutral and put on the emergency brake with her foot. Instantly guilt engulfed her. He said he needed help, not more anger. She looked over at him. He was stretched out on the other side of the car, his head loung-

ing back over the seat, his legs spread and looking as if they didn't have an ounce of energy left.

She'd been treating him as though he weren't
wounded, and he was. "Should I have taken you
to the medical center, Jaz?" Concern hushed her
voice, and she automatically leaned toward him.
"Are you hurting?"

"I'm hurting, all right." He rolled his head sideways and captured her gaze. Like slow-moving
lava, his gray eyes traveled over the contours of
her face, and his voice lowered to a raspy drawl.
"Hurting for you, lady. Real bad."

Before she could react, his fingers curled around
a handful of soft fur and drew her into a hard,
burning kiss. His mouth devoured hers, his tongue
plunging deep and taking her breath away. It lasted
a few seconds—it lasted forever—until he released
her and got out of the car.

Jaz stood for a moment in the open door, feeling the wind on his face, the pounding of his
heart, and the painful ache of leaving her. There
was only one way to make this work.

He half turned, and ducked his head back inside. Her hair had fallen down completely, tum-
bling around her face like a cloud of gold. Her
eyes were wide and soft, veiled with longing, telling him everything he needed to know.

"Hold that thought, babe." *You belong to me.*
"I'll be back." *To get what's mine.*

Chantal wandered through the rest of the afternoon, torn between bittersweet memories and a
languid sense of urgency she couldn't seem to
kick into gear. Jaz was gone, but that didn't mean
she could put her life on hold. She had to finish
what she'd started the night before.

She knelt in front of her hope chest and closed

her eyes. The tumblers rolled—right, left, right—but she missed. She took a deep breath and tried again, keeping her eyes closed. She didn't know the combination; she'd always relied on her fingers to tell her. Another miss and she crossed her arms over the top of the chest and rested her chin on her hands.

Jaz had said he was coming back. When? She didn't have a clue. Why? The answer flowed through her veins, filling her with anticipation and apprehension. She'd never felt before what she felt with him, a sense of utter inevitability. He wanted her. He was going to have her . . . if he came back. If he did, she was going to lose her heart.

Liar. She buried her face in the cowl neck of her dress. Lord, she wished that word would quit jumping out of her subconscious, even if it was the truth. Her heart was already lost. She'd done two stupid things the night before: stolen a necklace for her father and fallen in love with a stranger, a magical stranger who had saved her life and left her. The motives had been honorable for one; they were unfathomable for the other. Maybe it was infatuation.

Liar. "I heard you the first time," she muttered into the soft angora brushing her lips. She was losing her mind. It could only be love, which didn't solve anything.

He'd scaled one of her secrets, but not the worst by far. Nothing could compare with her guilt for leaving Paul, hurt and bleeding, on the roof of the Dubois villa—unless it was her shame for being there in the first place. Not even Elise knew exactly what had happened that night.

Chantal had been sixteen, and working with the absolute confidence that only the very young or the naïve have at their disposal. Like the gypsy children picking pockets in Rome, half of her safety came from being a minor, a time-honored prerequisite for a Cochard's first time out. If she had been able to get Paul off the roof, she would have taken the fall. He would have let her; he'd seen his eighteenth birthday the previous week. They'd been a team, equal partners, and she had abandoned him.

Partners. A heavy sigh blew from her lips, and her hand trailed down to the lock again. Foolish games, she thought, but this time it opened. She picked up the black pack, carried it to the kitchen, and emptied the contents onto the counter. Out of her junk drawer she pulled a soldering iron and a miniature tool kit. While she waited for the iron to heat up, she dismantled the mirror, putting all the bits and pieces in the drawer. It looked like anybody else's junk drawer, a lot of loose screws and odds and ends. The mirror itself slipped back into a wooden frame that proclaimed her cabin as "Home Sweet Home." She tapped the sixteen-penny nails back in place and rehung the frame over the sink.

With the soldering iron she turned the contact rig into a wire and two nondescript pieces of metal. All of it went in the drawer along with the tube of gel. She picked up the stethoscope and looked around her cabin. The whole place was a junk drawer, a mishmash of antique furniture, rugs, and . . . well, just plain junk. She carried the stethoscope over to the coatrack by the front door and hung it there. Hidden things were always more dangerous than the exposed.

Like her secrets. The slate roof had been wet, and slicker than the black ice on Highway 82 in the dead of winter. It had taken all her strength to drag Paul back under the eaves, where he wouldn't fall off. She'd stayed until he begged her to go, and as she'd run her feet had slipped in his trail of blood.

"Paul!" The hoarse cry ripped from her throat as lightning cracked the sky. Her eyes meeting his through a wall of gray rain. She clung to the tiles with icy fingers, her feet straddling the high peak of the roof.

He was slumped against a wall, his body a crumpled shadow of black against the white stucco. "Go, Chan, go . . . please . . ." Thunder rolled over his words, sweeping them away on the wind.

And she ran, ran as though the hounds of hell were on her heels, balancing on the crest of the roof and building speed for the leap to the garden house.

He had begged her to leave and never followed through with forgiveness. She didn't have the right to forgive herself, and she didn't expect Jaz to deliver absolution or live with her burden. She could take his loving, but not his love, not with secrets that couldn't be shared. If he came back, if he even offered her his love.

She checked her watch. Six o'clock. He'd been gone for four hours. Four hours of flight could put him anywhere. But she only had an hour and a half to get where she needed to be, finish her business, and make her date at the Hotel Orleans.

If Aspen had a dive bar, Snaps would have been it. Aspen did and Snaps was. The wood floor was scarred from the thousands of ski boots that had clomped over it. The heavy wood picnic-style tables were equally scarred—for the same reason.

Chantal sat down at the rustic bar, in full view

of the door and the boisterous crowd. In a sea of bulky sweaters, colorful parkas, and sleek one-piece ski suits, she stood out, claiming the glamour corner for her own with just her coat. She hadn't changed her dress, but she had repaired the Gibson hairstyle Jaz had so passionately destroyed.

"Slumming, Chantal?" the bartender asked. He brushed a pile of peanut shells to the floor before laying a cocktail napkin on the bar.

"Hi, Rick. I'll have—" she started to say brandy, but changed her mind, "soda with a squeeze. What are you doing here? The other bartenders at the Crazy Horse get tired of your stealing their women?"

"Can I help it if I'm irresistible?" The green-eyed blond flashed her a bright smile.

"Save it for the out-of-towners, Rick," she countered with a small grin.

"No secrets in this town. Keep mine and I'll spring for your soda."

"Deal. Have you seen Kyle Dawson tonight? I'm supposed to meet him here."

Rick put the soda gun back in its holder and set her glass on the napkin. "You *are* slumming. Or have you picked up some nasty habits I don't know about?"

"No habits. He's leaving for Cannes in the morning. He's going to take a birthday present to my father for me." Weeks ago she'd thought it over very carefully, looked at all her options, and decided on a private courier. Kyle was as private as they came, and he was headed in the right direction at the right time. He was also used to expensive cargo—expensive and dangerous. She was a lightweight, compared to his other clients. There were few secrets in a small town, and if you didn't count the tourists, Aspen was a very small town.

"He just walked in." Rick nodded at the front door.

"Thanks for the soda." Chantal picked up her glass and walked over to the table where Kyle had sat down.

Half an hour later she walked out of Snaps and headed for the Hotel Orleans. All she had to do was get through dinner and then she'd go home and cry herself to sleep. No, she wouldn't. She'd only cried herself to sleep once, and things weren't that bad tonight. The loneliness was worse, but the fears weren't as great.

Six

The Hotel Orleans was a historical landmark in Aspen, a holdover from the boomtown days. Small by modern standards, it emanated the intimacy and craftsmanship of a bygone era. Dark polished paneling added a lush contrast to the white marble foyer. Heavily scrolled archways led to the dining room on the right and the saloon on the left. A sweeping balustrade curved to the second-floor suites, supported by lightly veined marble columns.

Chantal turned left into the bar, knowing there would be an empty table in the farthest corner. Like Elise, Roger was a creature of habit and influence. She slipped into the red leather banquette and shrugged out of her fur coat, keeping the shoulders draped over hers.

A cocktail waitress dressed like a dance-hall girl who'd run out of material sashayed over. "This table is reserved," she said with an imperious toss of her brunette curls.

"I'll tell Mr. Neville how protective you were of his interests, dear," Chantal replied dryly. She wasn't in the mood for pretentious cocktail waitresses wearing too much makeup and not enough clothes. "I'll have soda and lime." She'd already discarded getting drunk as a way to spend the evening.

The drink was delivered a few minutes later with just enough force to slop it over the top, but not enough to make a mess. It was a very subtle gesture, and Chantal ignored it completely—on the outside. On the inside she muttered a few snide comments, realizing even as she did that her own emotions were what had her on edge. Battling wits with a witless waitress shouldn't even be on her priority list, let alone in the number-one slot.

She took a long swallow of her drink and lowered the glass. Okay, lady, you win, she thought, propping her elbow on the table and resting her chin on her fist. It was tonic, not soda, a not-so-subtle gesture. The day was holding true all the way into the night, all the way down the tubes.

Unlike at Snaps, her coat was no novelty in the Hotel Orleans. Furs more expensive than hers were sprinkled liberally around the saloon, which was fine with her. All she wanted to do was fade into the woodwork, close her eyes, and drift into oblivion. She managed the last two for a few minutes before her reverie was broken.

"Hello, Chantal." Roger leaned down and dropped a kiss on her cheek—which was as far as he'd ever gotten—and sat down next to her. He was dressed in Aspen casual, a three-hundred-dollar sweater, five-hundred-dollar cowboy boots, and twenty-dollar jeans. He wasn't a bad-looking man, just bland. His hair was thick and brown, with a slight graying at the temples; he had the prerequisite tan. But Chantal knew he could stare at her hard all night long and not generate the heat Jaz had with even the briefest of glances.

Chantal managed a smile. "Roger." She glanced

up at her aunt. "Elise." She forced into her voice a lightness she didn't feel, knowing Elise would die the death of a thousand swords before she let anything slip about the morning's fiasco. Lunch would be something else. Chantal tossed around the idea of calling in sick and letting an anonymous hostess relay her excuses.

"Chantal," her aunt greeted her coolly, and took the chair on the other side of the table, her back to the room.

This scene had been played many times before, Chantal mused, the three of them meeting for cocktails, dinner, and then everybody going home alone. Elise was between marriages and Roger didn't have enough nerve to ask Chantal for a private date or a kiss, let alone anything else. His aggressive pursuit of business deals didn't overflow into his pursuit of her, thank heavens. Unlike another man's pursuit, a man who hadn't asked, a man with plenty of nerve and the tender touch to back it up.

Elise and Roger began their predictable conversation of contract negotiations. Unslopped drinks were delivered all around, and this time Chantal got soda. Apparently the war of the waitress was over.

A band warmed up at the other end of the room, the guitarists running riffs, the drummer hitting licks. The saxophone player came in on a low note, and by the time the singer picked up the microphone, the band had melded into a tight rock-and-roll groove.

Elise and Roger's chitchat faded into numbers and names, and Chantal let her gaze drift around the dimly lit bar. A few couples got up to boogie down, and she noticed the warring waitress had latched on to better game. She was hustling some guy leaning on the bar, and, from the looks of it, was having a good time doing it. The sour countenance she'd subjected Chantal to had been transformed into the epitome of teasing charm, and her hand was practically in the guy's back pocket. Then, for heaven only knew what reason, she turned around and leveled another dirty look at Chantal.

Chantal immediately looked away, shaking her head. If she could elicit that kind of unbidden response from unknown cocktail waitresses, then this was definitely not her night. She tried to slip back into Roger and Elise's conversation, but they were well past the preliminaries, right into the guts of a transaction. She wasn't up to guts, so she concentrated on tracing damp lines into her cocktail napkin with her straw. A splashing brandy snifter put a screeching halt to the harmless endeavor.

The lady was good, really good, Chantal thought, truly amazed that the waitress had been able to slop two inches of brandy out of a balloon snifter. No mean trick.

"Compliments of the gentleman at the bar." The waitress sounded absolutely disgusted, but Chantal barely heard her. Somewhere, way in the back of her mind, the shape supporting that back pocket was beginning to register with familiarity. Jaz. Was it possible? Her pulse picked up and her heart lodged in her throat, but not before wrapping itself in a tight spiral of jealousy. No wonder the lady had been having such a good time.

She shot a quick glance at Elise and Roger; they were oblivious to the interlude. They were the ones who ought to get together, she thought fleetingly, craning her head sideways to peek around the retreating hips of the waitress. Her breath stopped momentarily, her teeth unconsciously capturing her lower lip in anticipation as she peered across the dim interior, trying to pick him out. It was predictably easy. He was the only man at the bar staring at her and mouthing the words, "Wanna dance?" He was the only man at the bar whose eyes met hers with enough impact to stop a freight train, holding her steady on a true course straight to her heart.

He was leaning against the bar, resting his elbows behind him, with one boot heel hooked on the brass footrail. Narrow-cut black jeans were low and tight around the cream-colored boots, and low and tight around his slightly thrust-forward hips. The narrow red tie and white dress shirt he wore under his faded blue-jean jacket added a rakish air of formality. He stayed absolutely still under her slow perusal, his body language open, inviting the hundred and one visions he put in her mind.

When she finally met his eyes again he gave her a long wink and a slow, easy smile. Everything inside her melted.

I'll be back. It was as if he'd never gone, which, considering the short amount of time that had passed, was a distinct possibility. There was nothing in Aspen for him—except her. "Ah, Jaz." She sighed, shaking her head with resignation.

"What?" Roger asked.

"Uh, nothing. I'll be back in a minute." She didn't know what she was going to say to him, but whatever it turned out to be was better said privately at the bar.

Jaz watched her approach, watched the tight sway of her hips and the supple movement of her legs beneath the clinging angora dress, and his muscles tensed with the memories of holding her close. The elfin princess was coming for him, and this time he wasn't going to let her go.

Old Roger didn't look too happy about it, but

then, he wasn't too keen on old Roger either. He'd seen the chaste kiss Roger had given her, and it had taken all his self-control not to go over there and show old Roger the correct technique. Not to go over there and take her breath away with his mouth on hers. Not to go over there and start something stupid, like a fight. It wouldn't have been much of one. The man had a good thirty pounds on him, but Jaz knew that days later, Roger would still be wondering what had hit him. Only Chantal's confession about no love life had stopped him. Old Roger was a fool. But moving too fast had been Jaz's own foolish mistake that afternoon. He wouldn't make it again . . . he hoped, his chest already swelling with a deep breath of anticipation.

When she stopped less than a foot away, he pushed himself off the bar and touched his finger to her lips. He didn't want her to say a word until he had her in his arms. Silently he led her to the dance floor, his hand trailing along the back of her neck, taking note of her tense muscles. He tried not to imagine all the ways he could work those tensions out—of both of them. But she had a way about her. Without even trying, she started an avalanche of hormones and other, more emotional responses that were both challenging and irresistible.

Right on cue the band changed tempo into a sultry song about love gone bad, and Jaz marveled at the amount of magic ten bucks could buy. Curling his fingers around her belt at the small of her back, he pulled her body tightly against his, until he felt every delicate curve soften and give way to his hardness. This was where she belonged. She had to know it.

Instinctively following his lead, Chantal closed her eyes and ran her hands under the collar of his jacket, feeling the warmth of his skin through his shirt. The sway of his body ruled hers. She'd think of something to say in a minute, as soon as she caught her breath and remembered how to form letters into words.

"I'm sorry for this afternoon," he whispered in her ear. "You left me hanging and I acted like a fool. Can we still be friends?"

Friends, she thought. The next step for strangers. Tonight she needed a friend. She nodded, and felt his soft kiss of acknowledgment on her cheek.

"Good. Did you miss me?"

"I didn't have time," she hedged. She'd barely had time to accept the hours of loneliness his leaving had brought, let alone share them, even with a friend. "Besides, I'm not sure you actually left."

"I left," he assured her, "but I came back because I missed you. Did you miss me?" The man was not shy about his feelings, she realized, and once again she felt the uneasy mix of apprehension and anticipation swirl into inevitability. More than friendship was at stake. She knew it as surely as she felt the throb of music through the slow ripple of the muscles in his shoulders, the firm pressure of his hips against her abdomen.

"You couldn't have gotten very far," she said breathlessly.

"I got to Denver and back today . . . but it seemed farther and longer without you." The saxophone wailed its heartache and Jaz swung her into a low dip, holding her off balance. A teasing smile lit the depths of his eyes and touched the corners of his mouth. "Did you miss me?"

"I . . ." She hesitated.

"Missed you too," he finished confidently, and pulled her up into his arms. The band quickened its pace, and he leaned back to grin at her, doing a gentle bump and grind against her body and shuffling his feet backward until they were lost in the crowd.

Incorrigible, she thought, feeling the more-than-friendly suggestion in each erotic move. He used the music to ply a rock-and-roll brand of sensual corruption on her body, promising more than he gave, enticing her with each added degree of pressure. Enticing her and drawing a response as surely as a pulsing flame draws a moth into fire; drawing her into the danger zone where desire overcame inhibitions. Words had no meaning under this kind of assault. She completely gave up on conversation and surrendered to his mating game, tunneling her fingers through the dark silky hair curling around the back of his neck. Tactile delight coursed up her arms and down to her breasts, pressed so closely to his chest.

His eyes held hers with a tenderness beyond the physical. His smile touched her like no other. If fate had given her this man, there had been no mistake. A miscalculation in timing, she conceded sadly, but no mistake.

"Chantal?" Roger spoke her name above the music as his hand landed on her shoulder. The dance sputtered out of her body, the magic faded from her heart, and she twisted her head around to look at him. "Our table is ready."

Jaz's hands tightened on her waist in a possessive gesture. His message was clear, and she knew not even passionless Roger could have failed to miss it. A faint flush pinkened her cheeks. She wasn't ready for a primitive confrontation, but neither could she pretend Jaz was only a stranger, because somehow, in barely twenty-four hours, he had turned into so much more.

"Roger," she began hesitantly, choosing etiquette

as the safest path of action. "I'd like you to meet a friend of mine, Jaz Peterson. Jaz, this is another . . . uh, friend of mine, Roger Neville." She doubted they heard much of the introduction under the music, which was probably for the best.

A firm handshake commenced and dragged out, and her blush deepened. This was ridiculous, she thought, but she had agreed—sort of—to have dinner with Roger and she'd made no promises to Jaz, not verbal ones, anyway.

She turned to Jaz and opened her mouth to say . . . what? Have a nice time in Aspen? Do you have a place to stay? Will I see you again? Nothing even remotely reasonable came to mind, and her confusion must have shown on her face, because he leaned down to whisper in her ear.

"Don't worry, babe. We haven't even started this relationship, let alone finished it. Have a good dinner." He stole a nip on her ear, thankfully the one out of Roger's view, and walked out of the saloon.

That would not have been her first choice of parting statements, she decided, completely unsettled by his confidence and the equally unsettling conviction that he was right.

Dinner at the Hotel Orleans had a lot of things going for it—fine food, good wine, and better service than the bar. But the best thing was their menu setup. They only served one entree per night, take it or leave it. That night's selection could have been hog jowls and Chantal wouldn't have cared less as long as she didn't have to make a decision. She was still feeling the repercussions from one she'd made weeks ago in this same dining room.

She moved the lightly sauced and undoubtedly

delicious *tournedos maison* around her plate, arranging and rearranging the shitake mushrooms between the two pieces of meat.

Roger waved the waiter over. "Take Ms. Cochard's plate back to the kitchen and bring her another." In typical fashion, he didn't check with her first.

"No, it's fine, really," she said, stabbing her fork into a broccoli floweret. If she married Roger, if he ever asked, her decision-making days would be over, she mused. Jaz had let her make plenty of decisions, and the only emotional blackmail he wielded was the sensual kind. In that department he made the other men she'd known look like rank amateurs. A very private smile softened her mouth.

"Now, that's the Chantal we all know and love." Roger gave her hand a squeeze. His voice was a grating intrusion on her thoughts, and her smile immediately disappeared. Yes, she silently agreed. He and Elise both loved the pliable, subservient Chantal, a role she was having a harder time maintaining. Jaz was a breath of fresh air in her life, accepting her decisions even when his life depended on them. The knowledge was a heady source of power, as was the potent desire that flamed between them. Never had a man made it so clear that he wanted her at any cost. No, Jaz Peterson wasn't shy. Her smile returned.

"Chantal?" Elise asked. "Will you take some papers down to the courthouse for us tomorrow?" Wine had softened the timbre of her voice. "I'll bring them to lunch." It had also softened the rather pinched look she'd worn this morning. But it hadn't changed anything else, Chantal thought. Lunch would be a time of reckoning.

"Yes," she said, getting a head start on her penance. Old habits were hard to break.

"Oh, look." Elise's voice rose to a lilt. "There are

Jimmy and Angela Sandhurst. Have you invited them to the Lodestar Charity Ball yet?"

The broccoli hung in midair, halfway to her mouth, destined not to get any farther. Slowly, with the utmost concentration, she lowered her fork back to the plate. Using all the skill at her disposal, she loosened her stranglehold on the utensil and released it without a clatter. She was ready for this. Right? She'd known it would happen. Right?

"Elise, I don't think the Sandhursts are interested in charity fund-raisers." Her voice sounded pretty good, increasing her confidence.

"My dear, everyone with money is interested in charity. It helps ease the guilt of having so much wealth among the starving masses." Elise flashed a sparkling smile in the direction of the Sandhursts and lifted her hand. "I'm sure they'd be delighted. I insist that you ask them. They are your clients, after all."

"Were, Elise. They were my clients. I wouldn't take their listing or business again for all the gold in China." A stubborn quality crept into her voice, eliciting a peevish glance from her aunt.

"Don't be naïve, Chantal. Business is business and, well, charity is charity. The ball was your idea. One of your better ones, I might add." The Lodestar Charity Ball had put Lodestar Realty on the Aspen social map the year before. Elise hadn't bought the idea of sponsoring the orphanage in Denver, so Chantal had kept her involvement private, except for the Palmers. Her aunt sometimes wondered, out loud, where all of Chantal's money went. An elegant, casual glamour, Elise constantly reminded her, added to the Aspen mystique. And when people bought in Aspen, mystique was a lot of what they bought.

Mystique, Chantal thought. Her clients didn't

know the half of it. No one in Aspen did, except Elise, and they both kept the family secret as if their lives depended on it. Certainly their livelihood did. Whatever Elise was thinking about what had happened that afternoon couldn't be as bad as the truth, and Chantal had yet to come up with an explanation. At least not one that wouldn't send Elise into a banshee wail of recriminations.

"Here's your chance, dear," Elise said sotto voce through a welcoming smile. "Angela is coming over."

And so she was, gliding from table to table in a bleached blond flutter of almost-kisses and -hugs. Dark-eyed and slender, except on top, she worked the room for every ounce of attention, leaving a trail of curious glances in her wake.

"Hello, Mrs. Sandhurst," Elise said. "I hope you're enjoying your new home."

"Haven't you *heard*?" An absurdly tiny, breathless voice came out of the statuesque woman. "We had a real shoot-out at the ranch last night. Absolutely everybody was there. It was just like the old West."

"Shoot-out?" Elise questioned.

Shoot-out? Chantal cried inwardly with dismay.

"Oh, yes! We were having a humongous party, when all of a sudden the alarm went off. The boys went a little crazy defending the homestead. Of course"—a thought seemed to cross her mind, looking oddly out of place—"it was a false alarm. Jimmy says there's a widgety glitch in the system."

Chantal doubted if Jimmy Sandhurst had ever used the term *widgety glitch* in his life. And only Angela would refer to five acres as a ranch, and a group of live-in thugs as boys.

"Chantal?" Elise turned to her. "Didn't you have the security system professionally checked before the"—a thought definitely crossed her aunt's face, looking precisely in place—"closing?" she finished lamely. The agenda for lunch tightened up.

"Yes," Chantal answered simply. Monosyllabic was her best bet at this point.

Angela fluttered a hand at them. "Oh, don't you girls worry. Jimmy said he'd take care of the problem all by himself. 'Bye, now," she chirped, and bustled off to the next unsuspecting table.

Chantal could just bet Jimmy was taking care of the problem. Her plan had been perfect, her motives pure. How had so much gone wrong?

The answer was three little letters—Jaz. Mexico looked better and better. He could have Cozumel and the Caribbean and she'd take Acapulco and the Pacific. That should be enough distance to keep him safe. If his luck held out.

Tense minutes of silence followed Angela's departure, leaving Roger with two women racing food around their plates.

"Is there something going on here I should know about?" he asked hesitantly.

"No!" Elise and Chantal both said, then snapped their heads around to stare at each other.

"I'm going to the powder room." Elise grabbed her purse. "Come with me."

"I don't—"

"Your nose is shiny." She made it sound like the crime of the century.

On feet of lead Chantal followed her aunt across the carpeted dining room, the marble foyer, and into the quarry-tiled bathroom. Her mind was blessedly blank, but not for long.

The door closed behind them and Elise whirled around, her face drawn tight, and paling under her carefully acquired tan. Her voice hit an ear-splitting screech. "Ten years! And a client! What is it? In the blood?" She ripped open her purse and started a frantic search for her compact. Tissues and keys were jumbled up on the counter. "No, of course it's not in the blood. Look at me. I'm a normal, hardworking—"

"Elise." Chantal tried to interject a calming note.

"—run-of-the-mill real-estate broker. Who had a perfectly brilliant career." The compact came whipping out, and their eyes met in the gilt-framed bathroom mirror, Elise's filled with raging accusation, Chantal's holding all the weariness of the past twenty-four hours, all the guilt of the last ten years.

An overwhelming sadness tugged at the corners of her mouth and pressed the breath out of her lungs. "I had to do it, Elise," she said softly, knowing the explanation was pitifully thin. "I never meant to hurt you."

She lifted her shoulders once in supplication, an action completely ignored by the piercing dark eyes in the mirror. Then she turned and walked out—out of the bathroom, out of the Hotel Orleans, leaving the coyote coat draped over a chair in front of a man she'd never love.

Seven

Chantal hurt all over, inside and out, and added to the pain by cursing herself for being a fool and failure with each jerky step. Sprays of snow kicked up in front of her boots, some making their way under her dress to melt and tingle on her knees, but she was past feeling the cold. Her arms were wrapped around her waist and her chin was buried in the cowl neck of her dress for comfort, not heat conservation.

Losing her job and listings was one thing; losing her reputation and her ability to make a living was another. She'd gone into the night before with her eyes wide open, fully realizing the risks, and she'd come out the big loser.

Fool. The word echoed between her ears in ever-increasing volume. No wonder her father had never asked her back. No wonder Paul had never written her. That Elise was going to throw her away like everyone else was a foregone conclusion.

Worthless fool. She knew she was being hard on herself, but anything was better than succumbing to the other goodies lurking in her emotional grab bag—sadness, loneliness, and pure heartbreak.

Out there, somewhere, Jaz was cruising. It wouldn't take him long to find easier game than she. A man with as much sexual charm and energy as he'd been lavishing on her didn't need to take no for an answer.

He was right: They hadn't even started this relationship, and if she had half a brain left after the previous night, she wouldn't let one start. She'd tried love once without sharing her secrets and had tangled herself in a web of lies. Her attempts to fabricate a respectable history for herself and her family had twisted and turned on her until even a man who'd loved her had walked away in frustration. Her wounds had healed, almost too quickly, making her wonder if she'd been in love or just lonely. Jaz Peterson wouldn't be so easy to forget. He'd shred her heart into a thousand pieces and she'd spend a lifetime trying to put them back together.

She found her car two blocks away and spent a few cathartic minutes kicking ice off the underside of the chassis. No coat, no job, no Jaz. Now all she needed to do was go home and figure out what she did have left, and she'd better start with a balance sheet.

Feeling only the slightest pang of guilt, Jaz juggled the containers of Chinese food in his arms, stuck a couple of the wire handles in his mouth, and picked the lock on Chantal's cabin door. With a little skilled maneuvering the dead bolt gave way, and he shoved the door open with his good shoulder. All right so far, he thought. Fireworks wouldn't hit the fan until she got home, but he was more than willing to take his chances. Some things in life were worth their inherent risk, and the night before, on a roof, he'd found one right under his nose. He didn't understand it, but he knew it as surely as he was standing in her cabin with a lockpick in his hand and Chinese food dangling from his teeth.

He set the cartons on the kitchen counter and made another trip outside for his duffel bag and a bottle of tequila. He'd stay out of her bed until he was invited, but he wouldn't stay out of her life—not until he knew Sandhurst had been neutralized, not until he believed her when she said, "Go away." She'd need a pretty slick line to convince him, and she'd have to deliver it with her eyes closed. There wasn't any room in her baby blues for lies, especially when he kissed her.

He filed that vital piece of information away and set about making a fire, finding a radio station through the bands of static, and figuring out how to work the microwave. He got action the first time and was feeling inordinately pleased with himself until the oven beeped and kept going. Not sure what was going on, he punched the stop button and checked the chow mein. Cold. His mother's worked a lot better. In a minute it could incinerate anything, turning a cup of coffee into a volcano and a muffin into granite, even his mother's muffins. Second time out nothing happened. After three more tries without being able to repeat his initial success, he rummaged through the kitchen drawers looking for instructions.

What he found was a lot more interesting: a burglar's arsenal. In the right hands there was enough junk in the drawer to break into Fort Knox, and he just happened to know a pair of hands that could do it. The lady was good, and her daddy had been even better.

The plans for a pilot-activated weapons system he'd retrieved from Sandhurst the night before had been a powerful bargaining tool, and he'd used it to the maximum and beyond, undoubtedly setting himself up on the wrong end of General Moore's favors list again. A small price to pay for the information he'd gotten.

A general's arms reached longer than the law's when it came to getting across continents and oceans and into files. Jaz knew the Cochards' history and their present situation, knew they'd only been caught once, knew her brother had gone to jail. He also knew Paul Cochard had worked with an accomplice that night. It didn't take much deductive reasoning to figure out why the beautiful French girl had ended up in America the day after her brother was arrested. She'd been sixteen.

Damn, Jaz thought. What some people did for a living was bad enough. What they dragged their children into was unforgivable. Elise was as clean as a newborn lamb, and from what he'd seen that afternoon, she wielded a heavy emotional stick when it came to her tainted niece. No matter. He'd take care of Elise in the morning. Tonight he wanted to take care of his lady, wanted to make things okay for her after the previous night's fiasco.

Given her set of circumstances and the skill to pull it off, he would have gone after Sandhurst too. The man played by those kind of rules. Life never turned out as neat and tidy as you expected. Sometimes you had to use your edges to get through.

The microwave manual lay underneath the junk, and he pulled it out and flipped through the pages, finally finding what he needed. The thing worked great once you got it out of defrost.

While the chow mein and sweet and sour pork heated up, he sliced the lime he'd bummed off the bartender at the Orleans, cutting it into eight chunks, and putting four of them in the refrigerator. He wasn't planning on getting drunk or getting her drunk. A little tequila would just soften some of those edges they'd both been straining.

Five minutes later he was stretched out in front of the couch with the paper cartons lined up on the hearth and the tequila bottle in easy reach. All he needed was a lady, a very special lady, and since she wasn't sleeping with old Roger she should be home anytime. He loosened his tie, picked up the chopsticks and the chow mein, and settled in to wait.

Nobody she knew drove a rented Jeep, and the one in her driveway was a rental, beat up but reliable—like Jaz. It could only be. He had a lot of nerve showing up on her doorstep uninvited and breaking into her house, and she was just the lady to tell him. Those self-defeating moments of melting in his arms were over.

She stomped up to her front door, letting each reverberating step harden her resolve, giving him fair warning of the hurricane about to cloud his horizon. Bursting through the door in a whirl of snow and wind, she caught him half rising to his feet.

"*Friends*"—her strident voice froze him in mid-crouch—"do not break into other *friends'* homes!" She slammed the door behind her, adding the perfect exclamation point. Mentally she gave herself a pat on the back for an appropriately dramatic entrance. Then he went and ruined it all with a cheerfully amused smile.

"Does this mean you're not glad to see me?" he asked teasingly, both brows lifting above his sparkling clear eyes.

"Don't evade the issue," she warned, tossing her purse on the table near the window and jamming her fists on her hips.

He'd expected fireworks, Jaz thought, not short-fused dynamite. Determination stiffened her warring stance and fractured the crystalline depths of her eyes into a hundred individual glints of steel. The elfin princess had turned into a Valkyrie of old. He was in trouble and thinking fast, but not fast enough.

"This partnership is formally dissolved, Jaz. Permanently dissolved. You know the way out." Leveling him with one more resolute glance, she turned on her heel and strode into the bathroom. That door also slammed.

A slow sigh whistled through his lips as he resettled himself on the rug. Once again she'd told him to go away, and once again he didn't believe her. The possibility of being wrong never crossed his mind. He bit off some egg roll and chewed reflectively, mulling over various and sundry opening lines for her return, searching for the right words, the right delivery. Something between a plea and an ultimatum would be nice. She might have been mad, but she wasn't a hard woman, and he figured he had a safe amount of leeway on either end of the spectrum.

Chantal was glued to the other side of the door, listening and praying. If he stayed, she was a goner. *Please go, Jaz. Don't do this to me. Don't tear me apart and ask for things I can't give.*

She hadn't left the room in anger as much as fear. The first sight of him had shaken her fury down to irritation. His absurdly confident smile had threatened even that justifiable emotion. She didn't have enough conviction to keep turning him away, time after time. Not when he continued coming back from out of nowhere to muddle her senses with just a look from those ever-changing gray eyes. There ought to be a law against that much persuasive charm in one man, that much warmth in one pair of eyes, that much sensuality in one body.

Only silence greeted her straining ears, and she knew she was lost. But she wasn't going down without a fight.

Rummaging through her closet, she pulled out a dove-gray cotton fleece jump suit, the outfit Elise referred to as "that sweat-suit thing." Actually, it had a lot more style than a sweat suit. The cuffs were knitted, but the ankles tightened with Velcro tabs and the waist was elasticized.

She undressed and ran a warm washcloth over the back of her neck, twisting and turning her head from side to side to ease the knots of tension. Then she washed her face and plowed a few more pins into her hair. She had planned on soaking in the bathtub until the hot water gave out, but with Jaz waiting in the living room she didn't dare.

After dressing, and feeling only marginally more fortified, she swung the door open and strode back into the main cabin. The best defense was a good offense, and she wasn't going to give him a chance to dissuade her, but he beat her to the punch.

"I brought Chinese." He lifted his chopsticks and grinned his most heart-flipping smile. He knew that finding his way to her heart through her stomach was a long shot at best—he'd practically doubled the contents of her refrigerator with the four bits of lime—but at least his opener wasn't a plea or an ultimatum.

Damn him, she thought, her mouth tightening in resentment. He was smiling on purpose, deepening the irresistible creases in his cheeks, tilting his head back to just the right angle for the firelight to burnish his skin to dark copper.

She knew very well that he'd brought Chinese.

The hot, spicy scent was wreaking havoc on her taste buds. "I already had dinner, thank you. Now, if—"

"I brought tequila," he interrupted, waving the bottle in a tempting arc.

Momentarily disconcerted, she gave him a dubious glance. "Tequila? And Chinese?"

"And I saved you an egg roll." He lifted a carton in the other hand.

Egg roll. He would save her an egg roll. Maybe food wasn't such a bad idea. It had been over a day and a night since her last real meal.

"And I have some more information on the Sandhurst deal." He sweetened the pot and his smile, turning down the seductive charm and going for pure innocence.

She could handle him, she thought with more conviction than she knew was sensible. On measured steps she rounded the sofa, plucked the egg-roll carton out of his hand, and sat down on the rug at what she considered a safe distance—as if there were such a thing where Jaz Peterson was concerned.

The first bite was ambrosial, crisp and crunchy on the outside, lightly spiced shrimp and cabbage on the inside. When she was licking her fingers for every last crumb, he handed her a half-empty carton of chow mein with a pair of chopsticks sticking out of the top.

Food did make a marvelous difference in her worldly outlook, she admitted, and she managed a small smile before slurping up a bite of the delicacy. While she finished the chow mein and started in on the sweet and sour pork, he twisted the cap off the tequila.

She watched with growing interest as he moistened the fold of skin between his forefinger and thumb, shook salt on the damp spot, and licked it up. His tongue picked up a few straying crystals off his lip, and he gave her a quick wink before tilting the bottle up for a long swallow.

His eyes squinted closed, and he gave his head one hard shake, sending a swath of sun-streaked chestnut hair over his brow. "Good stuff," he rasped out, coming up for air.

Concealed laughter shook her sides as he dropped the lime in his mouth and bit down. A few more shots like that, she thought, and she'd be able to handle him with her eyes closed.

Handle him with her eyes closed? Dangerous analogy, she realized when her imagination immediately supplied a number of mental visions of how she could handle him with her eyes closed—her fingers splayed over his taut belly, her other hand running over the supple muscles of his back and pulling him closer and closer.

"Tell me about Sandhurst," she said abruptly, banishing the images with the force of her words.

He pitched the lime into the fire, where it sputtered. Then he pulled his bare feet beneath him and scooted forward until his knees were almost touching hers. Handle him? she wondered. Maybe. Handle herself? That was the big unknown. Where had all her anger gone?

"He officially called off the alarm at the security place last night."

Jaz was much too close. His hands were clasped around the tequila bottle in the cradle of his legs, elbows lazily propped on his knees. She could actually feel the heat of his healthy male body radiating around her.

"I already knew that. I ran into Angela Sandhurst at the Orleans." As surreptitiously as possible she put the sweet and sour carton on the hearth and inched back a fraction.

"Bad night, huh?"

"Disaster with a capital *D*," she admitted.

"Has Elise put two and two together yet?"

"And come up with a perfect four. I think it's safe to assume I am now among the ranks of the unemployed."

"Did you hock your coat?"

So he had noticed. Try as she might, there was no simple explanation for leaving her coat at the Orleans, and she didn't want to reveal the truth about that messy situation. "Not exactly," she replied.

"Well, don't worry. I'll hire you. I could use someone with your talents in my business." And in my life, he added mentally.

"Sorry, Jaz, I don't see myself tracking down wayward wives in Mexico," she said wryly.

"I'll give you the husbands. There're more of them, anyway." She shot him a skeptical glance. "And it wouldn't be Mexico. I've been thinking about coming home."

"Home?" Her curiosity was definitely aroused, and this time she wasn't going to squelch it. Curiosity was allowed between friends.

"You're looking at a Colorado native, born and bred. Air Force Academy, the works."

"Air Force Academy," she repeated slowly, her sapphire eyes widening in admiration, or so he thought until she added slowly, "You must have *really* screwed up."

That was one way to put it, he thought derisively. Somebody had to get the ball rolling, and it looked like he'd been chosen. But she hadn't kicked him out yet, and that was the important thing. "I didn't think so at the time. You want a shot of this?"

In answer, she picked up the bottle and he handed her the salt shaker and a wedge of lime. What harm could there be in one shot of tequila?

she asked herself. And, she admitted, a shot of anything would feel good. The food had certainly helped calm her nerves.

Following his actions, she licked up the salt on her hand and swallowed the tequila in one gulp, one fiery gulp. Tears welled in her eyes, and she couldn't squeeze the lime juice into her mouth fast enough.

"Whew!" she gasped, imitating his reaction and adding a shimmy shake of her shoulders. "This is the good stuff?"

"The best." The absolute best, he thought, watching the shake of her shoulders ripple down to her breasts. No bra. The memory of her in his mouth tightened his gut better than any dream. He would have loved to see her small breasts and slender shoulders bare, with only a strap of something silky falling off them. To distract himself, to keep from moving in on her, he picked up the thread of his story.

"We were doing reconnaissance for a jet-fighter deal with one of our allies in the Middle East, real cloak-and-dagger. A few of us were kind of out there holding it together on our own. Looking back, I'll admit we overstepped our authority on the deal, operated out of bounds." Suddenly it dawned on him that he was still staring at her breasts. Grinning sheepishly, he glanced up at her face. An enchanting flush had stained her cheeks to deep rose. Either the tequila was taking effect or she was aware of where his mind had been. He liked both options, wanting her to relax a little and wanting her to feel the same tension that was driving him crazy.

"I was gung ho back then," he continued, "a lot younger. When the deal went bad, heads rolled. Mine was one of the first." Without any bidding the ancient memory surfaced, and his voice took on a sarcastic edge. "The military is real democratic about these things. They start at the bottom and try to lose as little brass as possible. General Moore saved me from the total disgrace of a dishonorable discharge. He understood what I'd done, and even why I had done it, but he couldn't condone it and he couldn't back me up. The problem was that *I* didn't understand what I'd done. I came back disillusioned, angry, and I headed for Mexico."

He slipped the tequila bottle out of her hand and gave it a long, hard look. "I almost drowned in this stuff, but I just couldn't quite get the hang of being a total degenerate and alcoholic. I tried"—a teasing smile curved his mouth and put the light back in his eyes—"but I didn't have it in me. I've grown up since then. It's time to come home." What he didn't say was that he'd finally found someone to come home to. She didn't want to run and he was tired of running. There ought to be a compromise in there somewhere.

"I guess we all make mistakes," she said softly.

"All of us, Chantal. Young, old, and otherwise, none of us gets through life without piling up our share of regrets." Maybe now she'd tell him what he already knew, share her burden and let him carry part of the load.

"How long are you staying in Aspen?" she asked.

"For as long as it takes," he replied cryptically.

Smoky blue eyes lifted to his. "For what?"

"You, me, Sandhurst." He shrugged, and winced briefly, his mouth twisting. "I've got to stop doing that," he muttered.

"Are you okay?" Concern lowered her voice as she rested the tips of her fingers on his jean-clad calf. "Did you have a doctor look at your shoulder?"

Jaz figured a man came into the world with only so much willpower, and his was slipping. He had to touch her. He picked up her hand in both of his and simply enjoyed the softness of her skin. "I made my drop at Lowry Air Force Base in Denver. One of the doctors there pronounced me ready for action, said we did a pretty good field dressing. I think I can get you the Bronze Star or something."

How did he do it? she wondered, watching the play of his strong fingers caressing her small hand. How did he draw so much out of her with the lightest of touches? All of her tactile senses pooled into her hand, signaling back the warmth and roughness of his skin, reminding her of other areas equally warm but soft like satin-sheathed steel.

Reluctantly determined not to remember, she pulled her hand out of his. "No medals, Jaz. Please. The last thing I need is to explain to your general what I was doing at Sandhurst's."

"I already did that for you."

The blood drained from her face, the muscles freezing in open-mouthed shock, and she waited for the grim facts of her life to flash before her eyes. Barely managing a breath, she choked out, "You what?"

Completely unperturbed, he grasped her hand again. "I explained"—he drew the word out, gazing at her patiently—"to General Moore, this afternoon, that I needed help last night and, as luck would have it, I found a free-lancer who knew the area and the layout of the mansion. I explained how invaluable your help was, how I wouldn't have made it without you. How he wouldn't have his plans back if it weren't for an incredibly beautiful and brave lady named Chantal Cochard."

The compliments didn't register, but something else did, like a ten on the Richter scale, rocking her to the core. "You told him my name?" she cried, on what was surely her last free breath.

"I wanted to make sure you were covered, in case anything happens."

"You don't understand." She jerked free of his grasp and stumbled to her feet. "You've ruined me, killed me." She ran one hand through her hair, pushing it off her face as she began to pace.

Jaz let her go, swearing under his breath. He'd forgotten that she thought she had secrets from him. And now was not the time to tell her he'd been digging up information behind her back. Nothing was going to happen to her. He'd covered all the bases before he'd started piling up favors. The bottom-line success of the night's operation had made him a valuable commodity to General Moore, too valuable to risk losing on a minor's involvement in a ten-year-old caper that had gone down bad without anything actually being stolen.

Propping his elbows on his knees and resting his chin on his fists, he watched her pace the small cabin, back and forth, barely getting her stride before she had to turn. Lithe muscles moved under the cotton jump suit, sleek and feline but definitely there, fascinating him on every whirl. Yes, he'd saved the general's brass the night before, and shortly after midnight he'd known what he wanted in return—the intriguing bottom swinging past him on every seventh step.

Unless he changed his approach, he had a feeling he wasn't going to get much of it.

"Come here," he drawled. "Please. Before you wear a hole in the floor."

Stark blue eyes in a pale face met his across the room, and Jaz wanted to kick himself for causing her so much anxiety.

"Please," he said again, patting the rug next to his legs. "Nothing bad is going to happen to you because of me, Chantal. Believe me." He'd make things awfully uncomfortable for General Moore if the man went back on his word, which he wouldn't. Jaz knew the military game inside and out, and he knew the man he'd entrusted her secrets to. If he'd had any doubts he would have winged it solo, finding out about her past through other means. The most preferable of which would have been her telling him outright.

But her eyes weren't buying his reassurances. Her legs started to tremble, and he watched in growing masculine horror as her face slowly crumpled up into tears. Oh, Lord, he could take anything except her tears.

In two quick strides he was wrapping her in his arms. "Hey, babe. I'd never hurt you." He buried his mouth in her tumbledown hair, his voice lowering to a husky whisper. "You saved my life. I'm only trying to protect you. I'm no fool, Chantal. I know there are things you haven't told me, but whatever they are, they aren't going to come back to haunt you. You didn't want to go to Mexico with me, so I put you in a position to cut your own deal, that's all. If things go bad with Sandhurst, we both hit the high road and let the military cover our tracks."

"You don't understand." Small hands clenched the sides of his waist; damp streaks of sadness soaked through his shirt and branded him with her misery. He wanted so desperately to make things right for her. She'd carried the past too long, a guilt and a heritage that never should have been hers. Not his elfin princess who deserved only sunshine days and nights filled with all the love in his heart. What her kiss had started, her tears finished. He was lost, totally lost, in love.

"Tell me, Chantal," he pleaded roughly. "Tell me what I don't understand."

"I can't." The muffled sob snapped the final barriers of control.

"Then let me help you forget," he murmured between a trail of kisses to her neck. He nuzzled the nape, inhaling her special scent, coming back to taste the tears on her satiny cheek. "Please, Chantal." He ran his tongue across her lashes, then brought her hand to his mouth and licked each delicate finger in turn. There wasn't a single part of her that he didn't want to explore with his mouth.

Damp heat tingled through the pads of her fingers and up her arm, corresponding with the hop-skipping flutter of her pulse. Long, rough fingers smoothed over her flesh and curled around the tender skin on the underside of her wrist. She saw his eyes darken slowly with the realization of what his touch had done. She knew what she wanted, knew what she shouldn't have. He was beautiful, gentle, and seductive, and he shouldn't be hers.

"Please go, Jaz," she said wistfully.

"No, Chantal." He shook his head. "Not when you look at me like that. Not tonight."

"Please." This request was even weaker.

"I'm staying." With his other hand he began pulling the pins out of her hair, letting the flaxen waves fall where they might.

"On the couch or the bed?" She was grasping at straws.

A lazy smile teased his mouth and shone in his eyes. "I think we'll have more fun on the bed."

"I meant—"

"Shh. I know what you meant." He tousled the last pins out of her hair and ran his hand through the silken tresses, giving them his utmost attention until every strand was free. Then he started on the buttons of her jump suit. "Chantal, listen to me. I need to sleep in the bed, with you, or I'm not going to be able to sleep at all."

The delectably full curve of her lower lip beckoned, and he bent down and brushed his lips
across hers. "I need your loving, Chantal," he murmured. "I need to be around you—inside you." He
slid his tongue in and out of her mouth, easily,
slowly, tasting the tang of lime melding with her
honeyed sweetness. And he prayed he wasn't starting something he'd have to stop, prayed that soon
all he would taste was her. "I need you tonight."

He lifted his head and watched the myriad emotions play across her face—a promise of passion,
a desirous need, and an uncertainty that tore him
up. The night before, he would have accepted
desire, but tonight he wanted more, wanted her
to need him as much as he needed her, wanted
no uncertainty. He needed her to say yes in all the
ways a woman could.

Her voice was barely a whisper when she spoke.
"Sounds like you need sex."

"Sounds like sex," he agreed huskily, knowing
he was walking a tightrope. "But it *hurts* like
love." He brought her hand to his chest and spread
her fingers over his heart. "Can't you feel it,
Chantal?"

She felt the strong, steady rhythm, the heat of
his body, and she felt his other hand slide over
her breast until he held her life pulse in his palm.
"Yes," she admitted so very softly. "It does hurt
like love."

Eight

"It doesn't have to hurt anymore, babe." His deep voice rolled over her in soothing waves. "Not tonight. Not unless you ask me to stop." His fingers played with the third button on her jump suit, and he captured her gaze with a burning light shining deep in his gray eyes. "Don't ask . . . please."

The roughness of his voice, the pressure of his hand on her breast, suffused her with a need she refused to deny. Desire heightened to a tangible entity with every moment lost in his eyes. It caught in her throat; it came alive under her hands.

She had known, long before he touched her, what the night would hold. Stranger, friend, lover, the progression was as old as time and new every time it happened. No matter the circumstances, no matter the briefness of the hours since they'd met. Love didn't have to be slow to be real, and it was never rational. It came upon you like a kiss on a roof, surprising and tender, pulling at you and never letting you go. Jaz's seduction of her heart wasn't meant for denial, not tonight, not when she couldn't ask him to stop. With a single tug on his shirt she told him of her need, and then she continued pulling the cloth free of his jeans.

The action swelled his chest with a heavy breath that came out as a shuddering sigh. His eyes drifted closed, and he bent his head and nuzzled her neck, moving his mouth in a gentle trail of sensation. Pressing his thighs against hers, he urged her back toward the bed, step by step, his skilled fingers undoing each button in turn, opening her to his touch. When she stepped up on the dais, he stopped moving and pushed the soft cotton down and off her arms, using her dominant position to gain access to her collarbone and throat with his mouth. His tongue laid a wet trail of eroticism across her skin, lingering at the top of her camisole.

"Pink satin," he murmured softly between her breasts. He raised his head, a languorous smile lifting the corner of his mouth. "You were made for me, Chantal."

"Are you so sure, Jaz?" The question came out breathlessly, her hands tangling in his hair, one thumb lightly tracing the bruise on his cheek.

"I've known it forever. It just took me a long time to find you. A lot of years, a lot of lonely nights. I'm not going to let you go." He kissed her cheek, her brow, the bridge of her nose. "All my dreams promised me you." A faint chuckle caressed her. "And finally, when I least expected it, they delivered."

In her heart Chantal knew that his dreams had promised him better than her. But fate had promised her him, for as long as it lasted, until he asked for a past she couldn't reveal. Unless General Moore traced her name to Paul's. If she never asked the general for his help, maybe there was no reason for him to pursue a name. Jaz had given him what he really wanted, and now Jaz was going to give her what she really wanted—his loving, to hold back the loneliness for a night.

She tunneled her fingers through the thick brown hair layered over the back of his neck, delighting anew in the strength of his body as he drew her close. "My dreams promised me you, too, Jaz."

He flexed his knees, and she felt his right arm slide across the back of her thighs and scoop her into his embrace. "No dreams tonight, Chantal. Only you and me and a reality that will put all your dreams to shame. I promise." He sat on the edge of the bed with her in his lap, her sweet weight more than a promise between his thighs. He tugged the jump suit off her, then rolled them back on the bed, pinning her with an arm on each side of her shoulders. "Or we'll do it again" —he pressed her back into the quilts—"and again . . . and again. Until we get it right."

She slid her hands up around his neck and ran his tie through her fingers until the piece of silk was free of its knot. "And if we get it right the first time?" Her voice broke on a whisper, her fingers slowly working down the buttons on his shirt.

"Then we'll do it again just for the ecstasy." Trapping her head between his hands, he lowered his lips to hers and thrust his tongue into the moist mystery of her mouth. She met each erotic foray with one of her own, rediscovering the taste and magic of Jaz.

When the last button was freed and she opened his shirt, he lowered the rest of his body onto hers, caressing her with his length in gentle surges that rocked her with an ancient song. A slow, coiling tension began where his rough jeans rubbed between her thighs, spiraling upward, encompassing all the rhythms of her body and drawing them into his.

Hot, wet kisses trailed down to her breasts where he teased her with his mouth, dampening the pink satin, and Chantal felt the coil inside her wind and unwind, pulsating with a need echoed in the unconscious movement of her hips against his.

His groan rumbled through her chest and his body picked up her cadence, pressuring the softest, most feminine part of her with the hardest, most masculine part of him.

"Jaz," she pleaded, wanting so much more. She pushed his shirt off his shoulders, taking care with his bandaged one.

He levered himself up and straddled her hips, shrugging out of the shirt, his gaze roaming over the delicately flushed contours of her face, the responsive light warming her eyes. "It still hurts, doesn't it?" He tossed the shirt aside, revealing all the dark, supple muscle and tight curves of his arms and chest.

She was incapable of anything except a sighed affirmation.

"For me, too, Chantal." He leaned over her and took each satiny strap of her camisole in a hand, pulling them down, trailing heat along the creamy skin of her arms. "But it hurts so good," he drawled slowly, his eyes half closed.

When the slippery pink cloth slid below her breasts, he inhaled deeply. "You're even prettier than I imagined." Incredulity made his voice rough. "I didn't think it was possible."

And even in her wildest dreams she'd never thought she could be drawn this tight, could ache this badly for something that remained just out of reach—until she did reach.

Her fingers grazed the path of skin above his jeans, following the edge of material to the snap, the peach color of her skin a sensuous contrast to the rich brown of his body. His taut belly jerked in as if she'd burned him, but he didn't stop her or reach down to help her.

She felt the shivering response of his muscles on the backs of her hands as she curled her fingers around his jeans and added the pressure to open the snap. A fundamental shyness kept her from going any farther. Her hands lingered in the gap between his pants and his body, wanting to touch, explore, discover, wanting to feel what she had only glimpsed that morning.

Sensing her hesitation, Jaz rolled his pelvis forward, increasing the contact, and his hand moved from her waist to lower his zipper. "Don't stop now," he said softly, "not when you're this close. I need you to touch me." Then, as her fingers smoothed under the waistband of his shorts, "Ah, yes, Chantal. Just like that and more."

Holding her tightly against him, he eased down on the bed beside her. With his hand he urged her onto her side to face him.

He was hard and smooth beneath her hand, and each of her touches elicited a low breath of pleasure from deep in his chest, giving her the courage to seek more of him. She followed the silky strands of hair down from his navel until he was fully in the small grasp of her hand.

Jaz stopped breathing for the longest time, watching her eyes darken past blue into a midnight hue of passion. Physical awareness of his arousal sent a glowing blush over her cheeks and softened her mouth. This was the dream that had seduced him through the shadows of sleep, but only part of the dream. The rest trembled beneath his hand.

With the utmost care, and with a strength born of desire, he lifted her body up with his hurt arm wrapped under her waist, and used the other hand to slide the camisole and the lacy scrap of her underwear over her hips and off her legs.

"Your shoulder," she said with a gasp. "Oh, Jaz, you shouldn't."

"My shoulder is not the part of me I'm worried about right now." A lazy smile graced his mouth. "Only a woman would remember that at a time like this, when she's holding something in much more need of care."

She snatched her hand back as if she'd been caught in the cookie jar, and her blush deepened.

He chuckled. "You're so shy—and so very, very pretty, Chantal. Worry about any part of me, sweetheart, because every part of me wants you, not just the obvious ones. But I'll admit some parts are more obvious than others." He winked and rolled onto his back, then kicked out of his jeans and shorts.

He was darkness to her lightness, with only the patch of white gauze, the pink on his nose, the crazy blond streaks in his hair, and the clear gray of his eyes brightening the all-over duskiness of his body.

The last remnants of her shyness disappeared in a wave of pure appreciation. "And you are so very beautiful, Jaz." She ran her hand up the corded strength of his thigh and over his jutting hipbone, the tips of her fingers tantalized by the soft-hard feel of him. "Where did you get this tan?"

"Mexico," he replied absently, more intent on getting closer to her, edging his thigh between hers and drawing her slender leg over the top of his.

"I meant this particular tan." She trailed a finger along the curve of his buttocks.

"I got that one in a very private place where I'd love to take you. Coconut palms, limestone cliffs, endless sea—"

"Oh!" The sound caught in her throat at the new pressure he exerted in new places.

"Don't panic, babe. I can handle this . . . a lot of different ways. Some of which may amaze you. None of which is going to hurt."

And he proceeded to do just that, amazing her with his mouth and hands in ways that would have made her dreams blush, amazing her with the more obvious parts of his passion, until she could hardly breathe and relief from the sweet torture had to come.

"Jaz . . . Jaz," she pleaded softly, her hands sliding over his sweat-dampened body, trying to hold him where he had only teased.

His mouth captured his name on her lips, stroking her tongue as his body drove deep and deeper, taking them beyond the passion into a fantasy realm of sensation. A realm where his elfin princess melted and tightened around him. A realm where he didn't die, but was reborn in her love.

In the soft hours of starlight before dawn, they loved again. Dream shadows played with the edges of reality, blurring the conscious and unconscious, interweaving the trails of their spirits into one.

"Chantal?"

She kissed his mouth and smoothed the hair off his brow. "Sleep, Jaz," she murmured, drawing his head back into the cradle of her arms. "Sleep."

"I'm hungry," he growled in the ear he was attempting to eat. Sunlight tracked a hazy pattern through the lace curtains, touching the dais, but leaving the bed in a veil of opalescent shade.

"You can't have my ear," she mumbled, turning her face into the pillows.

"You're the most edible thing in the whole cabin, my darling cupcake."

Shades of Little Red Riding Hood, she thought with a giggle. "There's food in the refrigerator. Coffee's on the counter."

"You call half a bottle of ketchup and four lime wedges food?"

"Crackers in the cupboard. Have a sandwich."

"Pretty fantastic, huh?"

Without any more clue than that, she knew exactly what he meant, and rolled over with a morning-after smile on her face. "Better than fantastic, Jaz, awake or asleep."

"Especially asleep. It was a religious experience." A broad grin widened his mouth.

"Well, don't go telling your pastor about it."

"You don't know Pastor Johns. He'd like my finding religion anywhere and anyhow, even in the sweetest lady the Lord ever put on earth."

She kept her smile in place with an effort. It was too soon to let the magic of the night go. She wouldn't think about the black marks on her heart, not now. "Last one in the bathtub buys breakfast," she teased, sliding out of her advantageous side of the bed and making her dash.

He caught her halfway to the door and slung her over his good shoulder.

"Jaz!" she squealed, and squealed again when he gnawed on her hip.

An hour and a half later they emerged from the bathroom. Chantal was still giggling and slightly embarrassed. The bathtub would never be the same, and the places he'd dried with her hair dryer didn't bear remembering. The man didn't have a shy corpuscle in his whole body and he was loving all the shy ones out of hers.

"Let's take the Jeep," he said, tucking the tails of a blue plaid yoked shirt into the black jeans. Chantal watched the last of his body disappear under the cloth and reminded herself to keep more food on hand.

She pulled a red star-splashed sweater over her head and mumbled, "Don't you like my car? Or is it my driving?" She drew her loose hair out of the cotton knit and pushed it off her face by running a hand along each side, turning the shimmering strands into two high-swept arcs around her ears. The sweater matched her pleated red corduroys. Jaz had chosen the outfit, going into a lengthy discussion and revelation of what elfin princesses wore to breakfast, lunch, and dinner. Stars were always de rigueur for elves, royalty or not. She had loved the analogy. As a child she'd thought she was a princess, always waiting for her mother, the queen, to come and claim her. But there had been no queen and no mother, only a picture of a beautiful woman on her father's dresser. At twelve she'd stopped waiting and started begging her father to teach her the ways of the Cochard men. She had wanted to belong. Last night she had belonged to Jaz, and, even more miraculous, he had belonged to her.

"I've got nothing against your car or your driving," he said. "I just look more macho in a Jeep." He zipped up the jeans and flashed her a devastating smile, his specialty.

She gave him a wry once-over, twice. "You'd look macho on a scooter."

They took the Jeep.

She directed him downtown, to a restaurant the size of a breadbox a block away from the Little Nell lift.

"What does O.B. stand for?" he asked, reading the hot-pink neon sign above the door.

"Only Breakfast. They open at midnight to catch the bar crowd, feed them, clean the place up in time to catch the early-rising ski crowd, feed them—"

"Clean the place up," he filled in.

"And catch the late risers, then close at noon. The waiters work a twelve-hour shift straight through, three or four times a week. They get great tips and a ski pass."

"You sound like a regular customer."

"Best-looking waiters in Aspen, and in this town that's saying a lot." She winked and gave him her own version of the devastating smile.

He crooked his elbow around her neck and planted a hard kiss on her mouth. "Just keep your baby blues on the boss."

With his arm around her shoulders they walked into O.B.'s. The place was packed with late risers. At a table set for four in the middle of the dining room, two chairs were occupied. Chantal led him toward the two empty ones.

When he realized where she was going, he stopped her and said, "This one's already taken. Maybe we could go somewhere else."

"Don't panic. Trust me." She tugged on his hand and slid into one of the chairs with a cheerful hello. The other couple said hello and went back to eating breakfast.

Remembering not to shrug, Jaz sat down. He had no sooner gotten his body on the chair before the waiter arrived.

"They don't mess around here," Chantal informed him.

Dressed as casually as any of the customers, and acting more casual than some, the waiter greeted them, or rather, her. "Hey, baby cakes. What's shaking?"

Chantal flirted back. "Hi, Peter. The world since

last night. I'll have a blue stack and one egg, over hard."

Casual Peter gave Jaz a curiously surprised look, and Jaz gave him a forced smile. "Whatever it is you've got, you ought to bottle it, guy," Peter said. "And save a little for me. What'll you have?"

"The same," Jaz said through tight lips. He didn't like his eggs over hard—closer to raw was more his style—but he didn't see any reason to keep Peter hanging around. The guy looked like he belonged on the cover of a magazine, but worse than his looks was his "baby cakes" routine. If anyone was going to be referring to Ms. Chantal Cochard in edible terms, it had damn well better be him, and not some oversexed waiter.

When he left, Jaz leaned over the table and whispered, "Remind me not to bring you here again, okay? And what was all that bottle business about? Has he been after you?" His eyes narrowed to gray slits.

Patiently Chantal took his hands in hers. "I'm the only local single female in the whole town he hasn't gotten to," she explained. "Sometimes I think these guys run book on me. If so, they've had a lot of losers." She noted the suspicion ease out of his eyes and the soft gleam of victory return. In another man that particular winning light would have disturbed her, but there was no denying that he had won—and so had she.

She became aware of the rapt quiet at the other end of the table, and, making sure she didn't look over, she released his hands and sat back in her chair. But she wasn't embarrassed. He was definitely loving the shy places out of her heart.

Only a few minutes passed before the food arrived, and Jaz spent all of them wrapping his legs around hers under the table, a very smug smile on his face.

"Two blues, hard." Peter landed the plates with a flourish and made a production number out of pouring their coffee. Stage aspirations, Jaz thought with a lot more charity than he'd given the magazine cover.

"Syrup, please," Chantal said, nodding toward the bottle at Jaz's side of the table.

He put a lot more effort into the delivery than she thought was necessary, getting up out of his chair and reaching across the table to pour it for her. She glanced up and found him grinning from ear to ear.

"I love you, Chantal." Propping one hand on the table, he leaned over and kissed the corner of her mouth, then turned his head and kissed the other. "I love you. I love you." Open-mouthed, he sealed his lips over hers and delved with his tongue, sweeping her mouth in lazy tracks.

Mesmerized by his words, she could only succumb to the undulating waves of pleasure flowing through her, and pray she didn't slide under the table. She barely heard the catcalls, whistles, and smattering of applause in the background—or the mad shuffling of plates on the table.

Finishing the kiss with a resounding smack, Jaz sat back down and noted the conscientious actions of their table partners. They had kept the syrup from running over her plate by shoving his under the stream.

"Thanks." He was still grinning wickedly. Turning his attention back to Chantal he said, "You'd better eat, babe. You're going to need all your strength."

Now she was embarrassed. And happy. And shocked. And sad. He loved her, and she couldn't lie to him. Sooner or later he'd ask questions she didn't want to answer. The thought made her want to run, a fruitless option. He'd been dogging

her heels since the alarm had gone off at Sandhurst's; he'd never let her run. That only left the
truth, and the realization killed her appetite. She
ate anyway, knowing she'd need all her strength,
not for making love, but for the showdown where
everybody lost.

O.B.'s tender blueberry pancakes turned to lead
in her mouth, bite after heavy bite. She kept working on them until she'd worn half the stack away,
occasionally intercepting glances from Jaz that
were turning more concerned with each passing
moment. She cajoled herself into a smiling countenance. She didn't want it to be over so soon, the
feelings of love, of being cherished.

Her smile was sweet, but weak at the corners,
and Jaz wondered if he'd moved too fast with his
declaration. After the night before she must have
known. That kind of magic didn't happen unless
hearts, and not just bodies, were involved. At least
it had never happened to him before. Nothing had
prepared him for the amount of love he felt for
her, this beautiful woman with the sky in her
eyes and the sun in her hair.

Declaring his love with strangers sharing their
table was one thing. Hashing out problems was
another, and he knew he'd have to wait until they
were alone. Maybe he could afford to tell her what
General Moore had revealed, let her know it didn't
change how he felt. Maybe now she'd understand
why he'd dug up her past on his own. The smile
slipped off her face as she pushed a bit of egg
around her plate. Then again, maybe not.

Jaz didn't have a lot of rules for living, but of
the few he had, not letting anything interfere with
his appetite was the one dearest held. Her unease
threatened to break his rule. He rallied by asking,
"Are you going to eat those pancakes or just fool
with them until they're mush?"

"Mush," she confessed, glancing up.

"Let's trade plates. You can play in my syrup." He made the exchange and dug into her remaining breakfast.

Chantal leaned back in her chair and shoved her hands into her pockets, watching him eat and wondering where it all went. Their lovemaking had left no physical secrets between them, and she knew there wasn't an extra ounce on his body. Every inch of him was a testimony of the perfection to be found in a man. That lean, muscular body, exquisitely sensitive to her touch, had excited and fulfilled her all night long. She didn't want to lose him.

With luck, they might not get around to the history lesson for a few days. The day before, she wouldn't have given two bits for her luck, but it had taken a dramatic turn in his arms. She'd grab every hour, every day, of his love and his loving she could get. Knowing what she had to offer in return made her feel like a thief, a real thief.

And so she was, she thought, reaching out and seductively running her boot up his calf. "Let's go home, Jaz," she said softly.

The three-tiered bite of pancake halfway to his mouth fell back on his plate as he shoved himself away from the table. Without waiting for the check, he dropped a twenty on the table. "Now I know why these guys get such great tips." He grinned.

Safely snuggled under his arm, Chantal matched each of his long strides with two of hers. In the time it took them to walk the block to the Jeep, the sun had disappeared behind a bank of clouds and the famed powder of the Rockies began falling from the sky. A group of teenaged boys on the corner howled their thanks, raising and shaking their skis in their hands. They whooped and hollered and punched one another as they made their way to the lift.

Jaz chuckled. "I remember when snow had the same effect on me. The thought of untracked powder was enough to keep me awake at night. Then I discovered girls. Talk about lying awake at night." He lowered his head and nuzzled her ear, pressing her back into the door of the Jeep. "Now I've got you, and being awake at night has become one of my favorite things, right along with having you make love to me in my sleep."

She turned her mouth into his for the warming passion of his kiss, her lips softening and parting. He took full advantage of her gift. His hand came to rest under her breast and his thumb tracked a lazy circle over her sweater, promising without delivering.

His unbuttoned jacket gaped open, and she automatically wrapped her arms around his waist, gathering his warmth and supple strength in her small hands. His body was like a furnace, so much heat in the snow. The waiter had been right, she thought. Jaz should bottle his magic. But you couldn't buy what he had in abundance, that tender touch, his special way of giving, the way he made her want to give in return.

He lifted his mouth from hers and kissed the snowflakes off her cheeks. "We can probably neck out here on the street for another five minutes, maximum, before I embarrass both of us. Or we can go home and start over again."

In answer she gave him one more quick kiss and reached behind her to open the door.

He grinned. "My thoughts exactly."

Nine

The first hint of disaster was the multitude of fresh snowmobile tracks on her driveway. Thin and more closely spaced than the outgoing tracks of the Jeep, they were easily discernible in the snow. The second sign was more than a hint. The cabin door was open.

They both noticed the breach at the same time, and Jaz shot her a disquieting look, the sensually playful mood they'd been cultivating coming to an abrupt halt. No snowmobiles were in evidence, but they both knew how easy it was to hide one in the forest.

"Stay here," he commanded softly, sliding out his side of the Jeep. He left the motor running and the door open.

Chantal watched, barely breathing, as he inched his head around the doorway, then slipped inside. Her instincts were to follow him. Caution and the knowledge that if they needed help she could give it better by remaining free kept her in the Jeep, for about thirty interminable seconds.

During those seconds a hundred different scenarios flashed through her brain, and she came to a painful decision. She had to let him go. Having Jaz hurt wasn't part of the risk she'd been willing to take. If it weren't for her, he would be in Mexico, working on his tan and chasing down unfaithful spouses, not putting his life in danger again. She had no illusions about her worth, and it came up far short of his life.

Sandhurst might be after his papers, but it was her home he'd traced them to. Reality time, babe, she thought bitterly, knowing the dream was over.

She eased out of the Jeep and sneaked up to the door, grabbing a piece of firewood on the way. It was a patently useless weapon, but it increased her courage. No sounds of a struggle reached her ears, which meant one of two things: They were gone or they'd caught him off-guard.

With all the stealth at her disposal, she edged along the porch, keeping her profile below the window. She took a quick peek through the pane and stifled a gasp. The cabin had been wrecked inside. Jaz was nowhere in sight, but neither was anybody else.

Feeling slightly less trepidation, she slipped inside, and was immediately captured in a powerful grip. Her foot came down hard and her elbow slammed back.

"Oomph . . . Chan—"

"Jaz." Her voice was a contrite wail. She turned in his arms. "Oh, sweetheart, are you okay? Did I hurt you?" Her hands raced over his body, touching, pressing. When she reached his seventh rib, he winced and snatched her hand up in his.

"We can play doctor later, sweetheart. Pack your bikini. We're blowing this pop stand, getting the hell out of Dodge."

Chantal's gaze roamed over the shambles, the busted clasp on her hope chest, the junk strewn across the kitchen floor, the disarray of clothes streaming from the bathroom. Every drawer and cushion had been overturned, and she felt a sickening wave of nausea from the personal violation.

"How . . . ?" Emotion kept her from finishing the question.

"The way I see it, you and the Palmers are the only ones living within a two-mile radius. Sandhurst knows you, knew you'd been in his house. It's not much, but he obviously thought it was worth checking out. Thank God there wasn't anything here for them to find." He paused and looked around the cabin. "They were thorough. I don't think they'll be back, but just to be on the safe side, I think we should take a little vacation someplace warm. Who knows? By the time I get you tanned all over, maybe the government will have pulled together enough pieces to put Sandhurst away."

He rubbed his hand along her nape and placed a kiss on the top of her head. Chantal barely felt either. Sandhurst had done this to her, torn her sanctuary to shreds, touched everything she owned. And as her glance took in each encroachment, all the hours of her past came back to haunt her. All the victories of generations of Cochards settled over her consciousness like a dark, heavy shroud, perversely making the future crystal-clear. The Cochards played by tidier rules, but the game was the same.

Bitterness and anger threatened to blacken the shattered pieces of her heart beyond redemption. She didn't fight them, not this time. She paid the piper, using her guilt as a shield, her love as a sword.

"Get out, Jaz." Her voice was flat and hard. "Get out of my life."

She jerked free of his grasp and strode across the room. Under the blankets, under the torn sheets where they had made love, she found his duffel bag. Against every mental command, her fingers lingered on the worn khaki canvas, the last touch of what was his. Her hand shook, and she clenched it into a fist around the leather strap. *Fate's perfect fool.*

Stilling her features into a blank mask, filling her eyes with indifference, she slowly turned to face him. Utter confusion slackened his mouth and crinkled the corners of his eyes. She tossed the duffel bag at his feet.

"It's been fun, but the party's over, *babe.* Get out." The razor edge of sarcasm was calculated to draw blood. She meant to hurt.

"What in the hell are you talking about?"

"You're the Academy boy, Jaz. Figure it out for yourself," she drawled, turning her back to him and flipping the blankets up on the bed.

"Look, Chantal, you're upset. Anybody would be upset—"

"Save the condolences," she snapped.

A long, heavy silence stretched out behind her, and her hard-won cynicism began to tremble and weaken. He'd shown her love, not brutality. But the best love she could give him was the self-sacrificing kind, and he would see any hesitation, any lies, in her eyes.

She gave the cabin a dismissive gesture with her hand and went in for the kill. "This is all your fault. You screwed me up at Sandhurst's and then laid a trail to my front door. I don't need that kind of help. In other words, no matter how great you are in bed, you're more trouble than you're worth."

Jaz summed up his opinion of her speech in

one foul word and came across the cabin for her, kicking the duffel with each stride.

She whirled around and flashed him a steely glare. "Back off, Peterson. I mean it."

With an action worthy of Pele, he flipped the bag up on the dais. "The luggage stays. I stay. Or you and I both get out. Take your pick, *babe.*" Granite-flecked eyes dared her to contradict him.

He wasn't making it easy, but his anger fueled hers, gave her something more to fight with. And she fought dirty.

"What do I have to do? Hit you with a brick?" she asked incredulously, lifting both hands, palms up, in a helpless shrug. "Hey, I admitted it was fun. You're a great lay, babe. But that's it. I've got a good life here, and with Sandhurst off my tail, maybe I can get on with it. Is that clear enough for you, Peterson?"

No, it wasn't clear enough for him. Nothing was clear, and it was all he could do not to reach out and shake her. The maddening impulse made his muscles twitch, turned his hands into tight fists at his sides. The royal elf possessed a whiplash tongue, and she had laid him open like a cat-o'-nine, cruelly, in his least-protected place—the part of his heart he'd given to her.

His fault? Maybe. She'd been the one with the mirror in her hand, but he knew she wouldn't have slipped up if it hadn't been for him, and he'd been doing his damnedest to make it up to her. More trouble than he was worth? Probably true. But together they were worth more than each of them apart, and it angered him that she'd reduced their magic to the lowest physical denominator.

Or are you the only one in love, Jaz, old boy? The first ripple of doubt drained the tension out of his hands as he searched the unrelenting depths of her eyes. Had he wanted her so badly that he'd fooled himself? Did he have that much naïveté left?

She held his gaze steadily, without any tenderness. What had made him so cocksure that she belonged to him? he asked himself. He found no answers in her eyes, and if there were lies, he couldn't find them, either, in the cool emptiness. Many times she'd told him to leave, and of all the times for him to start believing her, this was the worst.

He took one more look in her blue-ice eyes and knew he had lost.

"Okay, Chantal," he said, walking toward the phone. A pencil and a pad of paper hung from a string on the wall. He jotted something down and ripped off the top page. "This is General Moore's private line. Cut your own deal, but get out of town for a while." He came back across the cabin and shoved the paper in the front pocket of her pants. "A smart lady like you will be able to find me if you want me. Cozumel. I'll stay for a week and close up my shop. Then I'm out of there and you're on your own."

He raised his hand as if to touch her, but he didn't. His fingers were only an inch away from the curve of her cheek, and slowly they curled into his palm. He squeezed his eyes shut for an instant, blowing out a deep breath. The effort of his actions tightened his face with strain. Then he opened his eyes to a narrow, piercing gaze, his thick lashes meeting at the outside corners.

"One week, Chantal." His voice was harsh.

She didn't make a move to stop him, didn't open her mouth to cry his name. She flinched when the door slammed behind him, but it was the only weakness she allowed herself. Her feet remained motionless and her heart remained empty long after the sound of the Jeep faded away.

Noon chimes drew her attention to the grandfather clock. One hour until her lunch date with Elise, an hour she'd meant to spend wrapped in Jaz's arms, stealing his love, touching her mouth to his and making the world and the past go away. Instead only Jaz had gone away.

Pain incised her heart, just a small nick cutting through the protective layer of ice, but it was enough to scare her into action. She couldn't stay there and wait for the hurt to engulf her. Grabbing her purse and her car keys, she stumbled out of the cabin, pulling the door closed behind her.

Her fingers shook on the busted lock. "Damn them. Damn them." She forced her concentration onto Angela's crude boys. All it took was a lockpick and a modicum of skill. It wasn't like breaking a safe. Anyone could learn how to pick a lock. Anyone! It had probably taken Jaz less than a minute.

Don't start, Chantal. Don't start thinking, not yet, not so soon. She dropped the lock as if it were fire and ran down the porch stairs to her car.

"Do you want me to hold the Jeep until you get back again, Mr. Peterson?"

Jaz looked up from the papers he was signing and into a pair of blue eyes. They were paler, more like aquamarine than sapphire. Her hair was blond, but thick with a hint of red, not gossamer gold. Her nose was straight, without the slight upturn he'd traced with his tongue the night before.

Forget her.

"Mr. Peterson?"

She had freckles. Chantal didn't. He'd never seen, touched, or tasted skin like Chantal's, satin softness, all over. Especially the hollow of her throat, the tender side of her breasts, behind her knees, the lithe curve of her inner thigh.

Forget everything.

"Mr. Peterson?"

Jaz blinked and actually felt a blush steal over his cheeks. Lord only knew what the clerk had read in his eyes. "No. I won't be coming back." Chantal had to come to him.

"Too bad. I've got two free days starting tomorrow."

She'd read too much. "Sorry. My heart's already been broken once in Aspen," he said harshly, too distraught to hide his feelings. He finished signing his name and dropped the pen on the counter.

The clerk checked his signature against the credit card and handed it back to him. "Well, Jasper. If you ever get back this way, look me up." She smiled, and Jaz found enough of himself to grin back. No one except the military and his mother ever called him Jasper. Even his dad called him Jaz.

He slung his duffel over his shoulder and searched the waiting area, finding the bank of phones on a far wall. There was one more thing he had to do before he left. Actually two, whether she liked it or not. Foolishly, he'd trusted her with his love. He didn't trust her to leave town.

Chantal finished her second hot buttered rum and checked her watch. Elise was late, by five minutes.

She shifted in her chair and debated whether or not to leave. Maybe two showdowns in one day was one too many. More like two too many, she thought on a pained breath. At least she and Jaz hadn't been to this particular restaurant. Hell, they hadn't been anywhere except to heaven and back on an emotional roller coaster.

Lifting her hand, she signaled for another rum. With his appetite and her cooking, they would have hit every eating place in town before the week was out. If she stayed out of the Hotel Orleans, O.B.'s, and her own home, she could avoid the memories sparked by reality. The chances of her ever ending up on the roof of the Sandhurst mansion again were absolutely nonexistent.

The other memories, the ones brought on by a lapse of conscious effort, she fought every second and would continue fighting until his face blurred and the sound of his husky voice didn't echo in the chambers of her mind.

But it was too soon for him to be part of the past, and the echoes were strong and painful. *Don't panic, babe . . . I love you . . . I love you.*

She drowned the words with a long swallow of rum and pushed herself away from the table. Elise could take her apart later. She had to go someplace, do something, be with someone. Her feet carried her all of three steps before the grim realization hit her. She had no place to go except home, and she wasn't ready to face the emptiness and violation there. She had nothing to do. Lodestar Realty was off limits. And worst of all, she had no one to be with, no one who meant enough to take her mind off Jaz's smile.

Frustration evolved into distraction as she stood in the middle of the dining room, frowning and wondering how to outrun loneliness.

Mexico, she told herself. Run to Mexico and lie like your life depends on it. Take what you can and forget about what you can't give. The selfish thoughts insinuated themselves into her heart, pushing hard against honor and rightness. The memory of her own cruel words made her wince. Her need to protect him had opened up many parts of her personality, some very hard parts. Those hadn't been the words of a meek woman content to let other people or fate rule her life. They hadn't been words of weakness. She'd live without him. How long could it take to forget two days of your life? How long could it take to forget he loved her?

He loved her. Jaz heard the disembodied voice call his flight for the second time and still he didn't move from his chair. She'd told him to leave and he had believed her. He still believed her, but it wasn't what he wanted, whether the party was over or not.

How big a fool can you be? his pride taunted him. He rose from the chair and picked up his duffel bag. Pretty big, his heart quickly answered. With a groan of pure disgust he dropped back in the chair and covered his face with his hand.

But when the final call came, he found the strength to leave her.

"Chantal? Dear?" Elise waved a hand in front of her face. "Are you standing here for a reason? I'm sorry I'm late, but you could have gone ahead and sat down."

Chantal focused on her aunt. The time for reckoning had come, and she was ready. If she could fight off Jaz's love, she could fight the world.

"I did start without you," she said crisply, and

directed Elise back to their perpetually reserved table. She waited until they were both settled, then said, "I'm only going to explain this once, Elise, and let you draw your own conclusions."

So prepared was she for a battle that it took a moment for Elise's benevolent smile to sink in. "You should have told me much sooner, dear."

Elise was beaming from ear to ear, a rare enough occurrence to put Chantal on guard. "Told you what?" she asked uneasily.

"I've tried so hard to give you a good self-image. And when you finally do something absolutely noble, you don't share it with me." The barest hint of reproach crept into her aunt's voice.

"Noble?"

"Don't be coy, dear. Your Mr. Peterson called and told me everything. That's why I'm late."

The waitress arrived with a split of champagne—Elise always had champagne with lunch—and described the daily special. Elise ordered it and glanced at Chantal.

"That's fine." She waited for the waitress to leave and leaned forward, her mind racing in confusion. "Jaz? Called you?"

"Yes, he did, and he was quite candid with me. Honestly, Chantal, if I had ever dreamed that the Cochard area of expertise could be put to such patriotic endeavors, I might have taken more interest as a child. Well, probably not," she admitted. "All that climbing around and dead-of-night stuff never quite captured my imagination. And of course, in my generation, the women weren't nearly as involved." Elise took a sip of champagne.

The pieces fell into place, slowly, one by one. Even after her cruelty he hadn't abandoned her. Jaz had told her aunt a whopper, had painted her escapade with a whitewash of clandestine government activity.

Feeling an all-encompassing gratitude from the bottom of her broken heart, she went along with his game plan. He'd made it so easy for her.

"It was all very hush-hush, Elise. Even last night, at the Orleans, I wasn't sure how much I could tell you."

"I understand that now. I hope you'll forgive me." Elise leaned forward to whisper, "I'm so glad you didn't invite the Sandhursts to the charity ball. They really aren't our kind of people."

Elise had the world neatly categorized, and although Chantal didn't agree with all her designations, Elise had hit that one right on target. "No, they aren't. But I know some people who are." She paused, weighing her next words carefully. What Jaz had given her she didn't want to waste, not one precious moment of reprieve. "A whole group of people, little people without families, in Denver. They could use our help, Elise." The orphanage had been a touchy subject between them for weeks before Chantal had let it drop. She hoped her aunt saw things differently now.

"Is that where your commissions have been going?"

Chantal nodded.

"Well, if you promise to spend more money on your wardrobe, I'll double your contributions. Maybe we could throw in a ski weekend or two. Maybe we could have some of the children up for the charity ball." The idea took hold and snowballed. "Spring skiing will be better for them. Lots of sunshine. I'll get Roger to donate the lodging, and Lord knows we spend enough money eating out for a number of restaurants to reciprocate with food. You know, dear, this is just the sort of thing the television stations are always looking for. We could get statewide coverage for a project of this size."

Chantal breathed a sigh of relief and joy. She didn't care about Elise's ulterior motives, and neither would the children. Somehow, in all the muddle and disaster, solid goodness was coming out of her regression into thievery, and she owed it all to Jaz. She still didn't know how long it would take to forget two days, to forget his love, but she knew she would never forget the man and what he had given her.

Ten

Jimmy Sandhurst went down in the early part of March and set the whole town talking. The government froze all his assets and confiscated his and Angela's matching black Mercedeses and the million-dollar mansion. Aspen was no novice to scandal, but the sheer global magnitude of the Sandhurst case had the town crawling with national and international press, and Elise had to do her darnedest to restore a more pleasant image to the ski resort, trying to get coverage for the impending Lodestar Charity Ball.

For her part, Chantal was ushering children up and down Aspen Mountain, Snowmass, and Buttermilk. The little ones struggled valiantly with their skis, and the very little ones decided it was easier and more fun to scoot on their bottoms with their legs in the air. Or they just forgot the skis entirely and threw snow at one another. They weren't given ski poles. Anything that similar to a sword or light saber was just asking for trouble.

Chantal was also struggling valiantly with her memories. The news accosted her every night, reminding her of two days in January and one night with Jaz. Two months had passed, and she hadn't forgotten a single moment, a single kiss, a single one of his smiles. She wasn't crying herself to sleep, but every morning she woke to a damp pillow. Somewhere, deep in her subconscious, the memories were stronger, and during her dreams they controlled her tears. The magic place where she and Jaz had made love in their sleep cried for her.

The underworld of crime unfolded on the television screen and in the newspapers, but neither his name nor his face ever appeared. The omission didn't surprise her. "Unsung hero" was more his style. What did surprise her, and frighten her in retrospect, was the amount of danger they'd both been in. Jaz had known from the beginning and, undaunted, had plowed ahead to get the job done. The full realization of who she'd been dealing with would have stopped her cold long before she'd gotten to the roof of the mansion, long before she'd met Jaz.

But she had met him, loved him, and let him go, and because of all those things she was playing chauffeur to a van full of rowdy, sunburned teenagers.

"Swiss House," she called above the noise, and waved at Josh Palmer, waiting on the curb. "David, that's you, and Phillip and George and Casey. Everybody out."

The boys tumbled out, and Chantal drove another block. "Chalet," she announced. "Pammy, Kathleen, Diane, and Lisa. Come on, ladies. You've got three hours to get ready for the ball. Mr. Neville will pick you up at eight o'clock."

The girls filed out in a swirl of giggles and good-byes, and Lily Palmer ducked her head in. "Good day?" she asked.

"It was great, Lily. Thanks for volunteering to chaperone."

"It's the least Josh and I could do. If the original stick-in-the-mud, Roger Neville, can pull through with a bit of time and a lot of condo space, we can offer a little parenting for a night. How's that going, anyway?"

Chantal smiled. "I believe the stick-in-the-mud has transferred his affections to a more appreciative lady."

"Elise?"

She nodded. "Don't be surprised if wedding bells ring this summer."

"Well, even with the age difference, they make a fine pair. Maybe a younger man can hold on to her."

From everything Chantal had seen transpire during the last few weeks, Roger had every intention of holding on to Elise, and vice versa. "I think so, Lily. He'll be by to pick up the girls at about eight o'clock."

"They'll be ready. I've got four sets of curlers heating up right now, and Lana from Lana's is coming over herself to do them all up. Boys are *my* specialty, and I can't remember when I last used a curler." She tugged on one gray braid, then her impish smile faded. "How are you doing? Seen your prowler around lately?"

"Prowler isn't exactly the right word, Lily."

"Right." Lily drew the word out skeptically. "You borrowed Josh's twelve-gauge to scare off shadows."

"*Shadow* is the right word," Chantal said. "I haven't seen her all week. Tell Josh I'll be bringing the gun back."

"Okay, little one. I'll see you tonight." Lily waved her good-bye and went about herding the girls into the condo.

Chantal drove to Lodestar Realty and exchanged the van for her car, her mind remaining on the mystery woman all the way home. Shadow *was* the right word, a very elusive shadow. Looking back, Chantal realized she'd first seen the woman sometime during the week after Jaz left—the hardest week she'd lived through, knowing where he was, knowing she was only a flight away—but it had taken her almost four weeks to dismiss her fleeting sightings as coincidence. Had it been a man, she might have been more suspicious.

The woman was young, with the well-scrubbed, apple-cheeked look of a healthy college coed. Hardly a threatening countenance, but once Chantal had noticed her, it seemed she showed up everywhere Chantal went. In the weeks before the government nabbed Sandhurst, the sightings had increased and gotten closer to home. For fifteen days running, Chantal had seen the woman ski past the cabin in the dusk. That was when she'd borrowed Josh's trusty shotgun, strictly as a precaution. She couldn't begin to imagine actually shooting anyone, let alone a young woman, but the clocklike appearances were enough to put her on edge.

Then, as elusively as she'd appeared, the woman had disappeared and the Sandhurst scandal had taken over. Ridiculously, Chantal almost missed seeing the slender form kick and glide through the meadow each sunset—part prowler, part shadow, and maybe, if her instincts were still to be trusted, part guardian angel.

"Ridiculous," she whispered even as her gaze roamed the snow-covered landscape surrounding her cabin.

A plethora of new locks ran down the side of her door, and Chantal used a key on each one. She'd stopped playing games. She knew the combination to the new lock on her hope chest, and the only thing she'd soldered recently was an electrical connection on her new compact-disc stereo system. Business had been good, and for the first time in her life somebody else felt guilt toward her. Elise was making partnership offers and Roger had let her in on a commercial deal for the big bucks. Chantal knew they had misinterpreted her obvious sadness, but she wasn't willing to share the true reasons. Losing Jaz was a private pain, as their love had been a private pleasure.

"Captain Kelley." Jaz extended his hand to the slight young woman rising from a chair behind a metal desk. Her blue uniform was crisp and neat, the only spot of color in the beige military office. Her hair was dark and short. She had a helluva tan.

She responded with a smile and a firm handshake. "It's still Sally, Jaz. You haven't been gone that long."

"How's the old man?" He sat down across from her after she had reseated herself.

"Still a bear. Generals don't soften up with age."

"I came by to thank you for . . . for everything. The daily reports were . . . well, I appreciated them. I'm sure they caused quite a stir through channels, but I appreciated them." He was having a hard time meeting her brown eyes. The memory of Sally Kelley's perceptive reports and her sign-offs had made him wonder how much he'd revealed in their initial phone contact. As the noose had tightened around Sandhurst's neck, Sally had gotten closer and closer to Chantal.

"Don't thank me, Jaz," Sally said. "If I live to be a hundred, I'll never pull a better duty. Skiing in Aspen for two months! And to top it off the lady eats in great restaurants and knows the best-looking men this side of the Mississippi." Jaz felt a pang of jealousy as she continued. "I'm going to miss the Royal Elf and tucking her in at night."

That was the sign-off—Royal Elf tucked in and safe for the night.

Jaz had purposely requested a female tail for Chantal. Getting Sally had been a bonus. She was one of the best, but Jaz had known Chantal would pick up on anyone following her, and he hadn't wanted her to be frightened. Sally might have made her uneasy, as some of the reports suggested, but his lady had good instincts. He'd counted on her knowing there wasn't a threat of danger in the young woman.

What Jaz hadn't expected was the depth of Sally's intuition. After the first week, the private reports had gotten a lot more personal, and he'd hung on every word.

The Royal Elf is early to bed and early to rise, alone, every night. Methinks the fairy princess has a broken heart. Sandhurst keeping his distance. 'Fess up, Peterson. What am I doing here, having a vacation on the Air Force?

Breakfast at O.B.'s again. If Aspen ain't heaven, I ain't going. I owe you, Peterson. The investigation team is moving in on Sandhurst and I'm moving in on the Royal Elf. Tucked her in last night. She's hip to me, but staying cool. Sharp lady.

"Where are you going next?" Jaz asked. "Back to D.C.?"

"For a while. Then who knows? There are plenty of hot spots out in the world. General Moore might think I need a dose of reality after two months with the jet set. What about you? How's the private sector treating you?"

"I closed up in Mexico and cashed out better than I expected, and General Moore came through with a nice bonus." Jaz hadn't asked for double. Two nights in Aspen had meant more than any amount of money.

Sally rocked back in her chair, a reflective look softening her eyes. "She's a lonely lady, Jaz. Lots of gorgeous men hanging all over her, and she doesn't see any of them. I know it's none of my business, but I'm guessing a couple of free-lancers forgot to keep their professional distance. Maybe you should take in a little skiing while you're here in Colorado. I still have a season pass, compliments of the American taxpayer."

A sheepish grin curved one side of his mouth, and Jaz felt the Aspen Airways ticket tucked inside his new jean jacket. Sure, he felt like a fool. Still, he'd tried, really tried, to stay away. But he'd made it all the way back to Denver, and he couldn't stop now. "I'll take it, Sally."

The Lodestar Charity Ball was a formal event, a chance for everybody to dust off the tails and throw on the flash and glitter. Chantal had opted for more shimmer than glitter, in a cerulean blue silk jacquard dress, a little strapless number with a wide sash wrapped around her hips and tied in a flounce above her derriere. A matching bandeau tied around her head with the bow in front. The eight hundred dollars' worth of chic had been another gift from Elise, and Chantal had vowed it was the last expensive present she would accept.

The party was going gang-busters. Bouquet baskets of peach tulips and purple irises, white carnations and yellow daisies, festooned the lobby and dining room of the Hotel Orleans, spilling over on the buffet tables. The predicted four inches of new powder were falling outside, but spring held its own inside.

"Ms. Cochard?" Lisa and Diane, looking sweet in their semiformals, sidled up to her. Lisa leaned in close to whisper breathlessly, "Is that really Matt Whittaker over there?"

Chantal glanced at the teen idol, drinking champagne and leaning on one of the marble columns. "Yes, Lisa. That's really Matt Whittaker. Would you like me to introduce you?"

"I'd die!" both girls chorused, clutching their hands and rolling their eyes.

Had she ever been that young? Chantal wondered. The answer came easily: No. At sixteen she'd been running from the law and a life she'd never see again. It had taken ten years, the necklace, and a letter from Paul, but she'd finally outrun her past.

In an act of love Chantal understood now, Paul and her father had decided long ago it was best if they let her go completely. She had been young, with a chance to start over, and they had given it to her. Paul had had to live with his mistake. Chantal hadn't. Or so they'd thought. Many letters and phone calls had crossed the Atlantic in February. The Cochards were out of shady business, and the world was finally forgetting. Even her father had agreed that too much had been lost on one rainy night, and he was finding it sufficient to battle wits with his legitimate customers.

There had been one other price to pay for her freedom—the love of Jaz—and she was still making those payments every night in her dreams. She didn't know where he was, but she had memorized the phone number he'd shoved in her pocket. *Washington D.C., General Moore, my name is Jaz Peterson. My name is Jaz . . .*

"I promise you won't die," she said to the girls. "He's a nice man. Come on." She took each of the girls by the hand and felt their fingers close tightly around hers. Some celebrities were approachable and some were not. Fortunately Matt Whittaker was of the former, still young enough and new enough to truly enjoy his fame.

Matt noticed their approach and put on the million-dollar smile. "Hi, Chantal." The little hands almost crushed her fingers.

"Hi, Matt. By some miracle I found a couple of your fans at the party. Lisa Dunn and Diane Fransen. You *are* fans, aren't you?" She gave the girls an opening line, knowing the first words were always the hardest.

"Oh, yes."

"We've seen all your movies," Diane gushed.

"Both of them?" Matt smiled at each of them in turn.

"Oh, yes. *Vagabonds* we saw three times. Didn't we, Diane?"

"At least three times. And *Into the Sky* twice."

"*Vagabonds* was my favorite too," Matt said.

Chantal eased away quietly. Matt might be young, but he had enough moves to get out of the conversation when he was ready. She looked around the dining room and found the boys all lined up at the buffet table, eating as though there were no tomorrow. Pammy and Kathleen were talking with the Palmers and two of their sons. With all her charges entertained, Chantal took a moment to slip into the bar to check on the other guests.

"Valet parking," Jaz muttered, and looked down at his plain white shirt, skinny red tie, and black wool pleated slacks. He glanced back at his suit jacket, draped over the jump seat of the Jeep, then up at the tuxedoed valet standing in front of the Hotel Orleans. It was too late to get a tuxedo. He'd have to make do.

He passed the Orleans and ended up parking four blocks away. Walking the first two blocks was easy, and he did it with long, sure strides. The third block slowed him down a bit, and it wasn't because of the snow sliding under his cowboy boots. The fourth block became an absolute mosey.

He'd told her a week and given her eight, eight of the lousiest weeks of his life. He stopped and shoved his hands deep into his pants pockets, pushing back the panels of his jacket. So what in the hell are you doing here? he asked himself.

Eight weeks of no love and damn little sleep. The dreams had haunted him more than the waking memories. Traveling two thousand miles for a decent night's sleep was about the feeblest scheme he'd ever had, especially when the plan lacked any guarantees.

So when did love ever come with guarantees? For that matter, when did life ever come with guarantees? Besides, he'd decided two days earlier that it couldn't get any worse than it already was, even if she kicked him out again.

He brushed the snow off his shoulders and started walking again, concentrating on how he was going to get into the high-class party. Approaching Chantal would have to be winged, one of those seat-of-your-emotional-pants things he'd gotten so good at with her.

Two valets, one doorman. It could have been worse. There could have been an armed guard. It could have been easier. He could have had an engraved invitation.

Then the winds of fate blew him a gift in the form of one of the valets, six feet two inches of dazzling smile and coal-black hair.

"Hi, Peter. Moonlighting?" Jaz hadn't forgotten a moment, a place, or a name from his time with Chantal.

"Not exactly. O.B.'s donated me for the night," Peter replied easily. "It's not all bad, though. They auction off the bachelors later, and I should be good for a grand or—Hey, I remember you."

"Good."

"Yeah, the guys and I started a fan club. We were having trouble getting action on Chantal, but you really put some life back in the game."

Some people really deserved to have their too-perfect faces rearranged, Jaz thought, and this guy was at the top of his list. But breaking the nose of somebody you needed a favor from wasn't considered a smart move in any crowd.

"Well, I'm running my own action tonight," he said, "and I need to get in. Can you do it?" He slipped Peter a fifty, figuring the guy's sizable ego should do the rest. People with the least weight to shove around usually liked to shove it around the most.

"No problema, amigo." Peter pocketed the bill with a flashy smile.

The jerk probably had "bilingual" on his resume, Jaz thought. He refrained from a barrio comeback that would cast doubts on the waiter's sexual prowess, and said only, *"Gracias."*

Peter walked over to the doorman and said something to him, then returned after a long minute. "If you've got this guy's twin"—he patted his pocket—"Jerry says you're in."

"No problema, amigo." Jaz thumbed another fifty off his roll, handed it to the doorman, and walked in as if he owned the place.

Just inside the door he snapped a white carnation off a bouquet and put it in his lapel buttonhole. Halfway across the lobby he snagged a glass of champagne off the tray of a passing waiter. Then he started cruising.

• • •

Chantal leaned on the bar. "Hi, Rick. I'll have a soda and lime."

"The champagne's free."

"So's the soda." She smiled. "Did the other bartenders at Snaps get tired of your stealing—"

"Déjà vu," he interrupted, grinning. "No. I'm Snaps's donation. They're counting on me to set a new record at the bachelor auction."

"Good luck. O.B.'s sent three of their hottest numbers over."

"O.B.'s," he said with a snort. "Those guys don't have any class. No style. I'm counting on the good ladies of Aspen to have an appreciation for my subtle charm."

"Subtle like a freight train," Chantal teased.

His sea-green eyes lit up like twin candles at her flirtatious comment. "Of course," he drawled, "I can be had for a lot less . . . by the right lady." He leaned across the bar and turned up the heat of his charm.

"Save it—"

"—for the out-of-towners. Gotcha." He flipped a glass in the air and caught it before making her soda and lime.

"Thanks." Chantal accepted the drink and wandered back into the lobby.

Jaz saw her first, and his heart plunged toward the marble floor, along with every ounce of confidence he'd been building up. Svelteness, femininity, sweet curves, and legs that went all the way. That dress made his mouth go dry and his imagination run wild. She looked like an imported delicacy, pure sensual delight wrapped in a shimmer of blue silk, complete with bows. Had he really held her? Made love to her? Or had it all been a dream?

What his mind doubted, his body remembered, powerfully—every taste, touch, and scent. He turned away to catch his breath, but her image remained. The shape of her mouth, especially the fullness of her lower lip; the slope of her shoulders, especially bare; and her hair, silver-gold and finer than silk, especially as he ran his hands through it when he kissed her. All these things went through his mind while he stared sightlessly at the floor.

"Mr. Peterson?"

Jaz glanced up, and if it was possible, his heart sank even lower. "Ms. Stahl," he choked out.

"I thought I recognized you. I didn't realize Chantal had invited you." There goes a hundred bucks, he thought. "But I'm terribly glad she did."

Jaz kept his total confusion to himself and lightly grasped her extended hand. "I wouldn't have missed it for anything."

"I did as you asked, and kept a very close eye on Chantal these last few weeks. Of course, I don't expect any *official* acknowledgment." Her tone implied the opposite. "I'm so pleased your investigation was successful. The scandal is awful, but Aspen will survive. We always do."

Jaz was doing a mental hundred-yard dash, wondering if he could squeeze one more favor out of General Moore. How much could a phone call cost him in the favors department? Certainly not as much as an honorable discharge. That one had ended up costing him his heart. He forced himself not to look around.

"Are you married, Mr. Peterson?" Elise continued.

Coming from his, he hoped, future aunt-in-law, the question threw him. "No," he managed in a gruff voice.

"Well, then, you really must participate in our bachelor auction. It's all for charity. We're spotlighting an orphanage in Denver this year. Some of the little orphans are here."

"I don't think so, Ms. Stahl. I've seen the competition."

"Don't be coy, Mr. Peterson. I'm sure you'll hold your own. The O.B. boys are here, but only three of them."

Jaz thought that was a compliment, but he wasn't sure, so he ignored it. "I'll be happy to make a donation, but no auction." He would never, ever recover if Chantal didn't bid on him, or, worse, bid on one of the O.B. jerks. Lord, was love always like this? Ego-destroying? What had happened to the ever-confident man he used to be?

"I can see I'm going to need some help on this," Elise said. Her gaze traveled over his shoulder. "Chantal? Dear?" she called. "Would you come over, please?"

Jaz sucked in a breath through his teeth and tried to steel himself, but it was damn near impossible to steel yourself when all your insides were bouncing off one another.

Eleven

Chantal caught Elise's gesture out of the corner of her eye and was immediately distracted by Lisa and Diane.

"Oh, Ms. Cochard. Matt's so nice. Thank you so much."

"Oh, yes. Thank you," Lisa piped up. The faces of both were flushed, their eyes bright.

"You're welcome." Chantal grasped each of their hands in turn and took a step back toward Elise, accidentally bumping into another guest.

"Oops, sorry."

"Great party." The woman smiled and moved on.

A really great party, Chantal silently agreed, working her way through the crowd. Three hundred tickets at two hundred dollars apiece had already put them over the last year's total, and they still had the bachelor auction ahead of them. Roger, of all people, had dreamed up the idea. The O.B. men should be good for a few grand for charity, Chantal mused. Lord knew how much money would change hands privately after the bidding was over. She knew Peter was taking on all comers for the highest bid. Somebody could do that guy a real favor by breaking his nose and making him rely more on what he had inside instead of his looks.

Another O.B. waiter passed her with a tray of empty glasses and gave her a quick update on the champagne supply.

"Rick has another five cases in the bar," she informed him with a smile, wondering if Peter really had given the competition realistic odds. The outcome of the auction would have tongues wagging for months. The whole party would. Personally, to her it felt like a culmination and a beginning at the same time. She would never abandon the orphanage, but after tonight her contributions would be made out of love, not guilt. *A smart lady like you will be able to find me if you want me.*

She took the time to shake one more hand and accept one more round of congratulations before turning to take the last step toward her aunt. "Hi, Elise. I—" She glanced up to include Elise's conversation partner and the rest of her words floated off in a soundless breath of air. She blinked once, twice, and he was still there, gazing down at her with river-clear eyes, his expression tender and unsure. Good grief! Had she conjured him up out of her thoughts?

"You remember Mr. Peterson, don't you, Chantal? Of course you do. It was so thoughtful of you to invite him."

Chantal lifted her hand in an automatic gesture. A flood of memories returned with his touch: the roughness of his hands, the gentleness of his caresses, the surprising heat of his body. He was real, wonderfully, miraculously real.

"I've asked him to participate in the bachelor

auction," Elise continued, "but he's balking. Maybe you can convince him."

His nose wasn't peeling anymore, she saw, but the sun streaks were still woven through his dark hair. It still swept across the tops of his ears and layered around the back of his neck, so much thick silk waiting to be explored by her fingers. The smile creases in his cheeks were shallow, with a lack of expression, but his eyes were soft with longing, the same longing tightening her chest and catching her breath.

"I've explained it's all for charity," Elise was saying, "but Mr. Peterson seems a little shy. I've assured him he'll carry his weight. The fresh, outdoor look always goes over well in Aspen."

So did broad shoulders, lanky, muscular bodies, and teasing smiles. She couldn't throw him away again, didn't have that much nobleness left. Loneliness and damp pillows had soaked all the magnanimity out of her heart, and Paul had given her back an unblemished soul. Nothing could change the past, but if Jaz had come back for her once more, after the terrible things she'd said, maybe, just maybe, he loved her enough to understand. It was a chance she had no choice but to take.

Chantal slowly turned her gaze to Elise, her hand still clasped in Jaz's. "No, I don't think auctioning Mr. Peterson is a good idea. I'll . . . uh, write you a check in the morning."

His hand tightened around hers possessively, and a surprisingly shy smile curved his mouth and warmed the depths of his eyes. "I think we can work something out without resorting to cash." His voice was deep and soft.

Whether it was his smile or his words, Chantal didn't know, but her confidence tripled. She'd give their love every chance possible. "Elise? Can you and the crew handle the auction without me?"

"I think we're going to have to." Remarkably, Elise didn't seem at all perturbed.

Chantal lifted her eyes to Jaz. "I need to get my coat. Did you check yours?"

"I didn't need one."

"No." She laughed softly. "I guess you wouldn't."

Hand in hand, they ascended the sweeping marble staircase to the suite reserved for the party organizers, their only communication being the slow entwining of their fingers. The room was dark, but when Jaz reached for the light switch Chantal stopped him by turning in his arms and pressing her body close to his. She needed to feel him, kiss him, have him kiss her.

"I missed you," she whispered, resting his hand on her hip. She raised herself on tiptoe to reach his mouth and lightly brushed her lips across his, wrapping her arms around his neck. "I missed you so much, Jaz. My heart broke every night with wanting you."

"Chan . . ." He pulled her close. "Why didn't you come? If you hurt as badly as I did, why didn't you come?"

She rubbed her nose down the side of his, inhaling the warm scent of him, letting it suffuse her senses. "I loved you too much, Jaz."

Jaz mulled that over between kisses and didn't come up with much. He chalked it up to the inscrutable female psyche and continued his delightful exploration of the utterly feminine woman in his arms. She loved him. The wonder of it filled him with passionate need and sweet serenity.

Her tongue traced his lips, tasting and giving until he captured her mouth and brought them both the magic they needed. His arms tightened around her and lifted her off the floor, giving them greater access to touch and tease and remember.

Like a thief in the night, she stole the wild passion of his kiss, one moment rough and hard and the next so soft and gentle. She led him on and on, layering soft bites along his jaw and coming back to play with his mouth. His low groan echoed across her lips, and she felt his body tense and harden. How had she ever let him go, this other part of her?

"Chan . . . let's get out of here. Where's your coat?"

"In the bedroom," she murmured, sliding out of his arms.

"Bedroom?" he repeated hopefully.

She shook her head and gave his hand a squeeze before releasing him. "At least ten other people have a key to this suite."

"Right," he agreed. "Let's get your coat and go home."

He helped her sort through the pile of minks and foxes to find the coyote fur. "Are you going to tell me what happened to this coat that other night at the Orleans?" he asked, helping her into it.

She hooked the clasps running down the front and looked up at him. "I'm going to tell you everything, Jaz."

"Even the part about loving me so much, you broke my heart?"

"Especially that part." He had a right to know, and she needed him to know. She didn't want any lies between them, even if telling the truth meant losing him.

It took fifteen minutes' worth of good-byes to traverse the lobby, and when they finally made it to the door Chantal glanced out at the snow and then down at her blue satin heels. "I forgot my boots," she said, sighing in frustration. The waiting to be in his arms again and the waiting to tell him the truth were tying her emotions in knots. She hadn't decided which course of action to pursue first. Nobleness required the truth, but, as she'd discovered earlier, her nobleness was in short supply that evening.

"Nothing is going to get me back across that lobby, babe," Jaz said, lifting her up in his arms. "We'll make do. Comfy?"

"This is the best I've felt in months." She smiled and wrapped her arms around his neck. "How's your shoulder?"

"Better than new. And you're right, you feel great." He nuzzled his mouth close to her ear and whispered huskily, "But you're going to feel a lot better when I get you home. And me, too, better all over."

The warmth of his breath and his words sent a heat wave straight down the middle of her body, and Chantal felt her nobleness slip a dozen notches all at once. She tunneled her fingers through the dark hair brushing his collar and raised her eyes to meet his. "Take me home, Jaz."

He shoved through the door and nodded at Peter, who took one look at them and turned to the doorman. "Pay up, Jerry. I told you, we could all learn something from this guy."

Jaz halted in mid-stride. "Do you want me to hit him?" he asked Chantal.

"No. We need him for the bachelor auction. But if he ever runs book on me again, you can take him out."

He grinned. "You've got a deal, partner."

He carried her down the street, and by the time they reached the third block she said, "They're only shoes, Jaz. Maybe I should walk. I don't want you to wear yourself out."

Without stopping he replied, "If you knew what my body is doing, you'd be praying I'd get a little worn out before I get you home."

She snuggled up closer and laid her mouth on his ear. "Oh, I know what you're feeling, Jaz. I'm feeling it too."

"Then I really don't know how you stayed away. For that matter I don't know why you kicked me out in the first place—or why I let you." They reached the Jeep, but rather than setting her down, he tightened his arms around her. "Why *did* you kick me out? Don't tell me you meant the things you said, because I figured out about half-way to Mexico that it was a line of bull. Problem was, I knew you'd said them for a reason. I never doubted that you wanted me to leave. I just never figured out why. Was I moving too fast?"

She hedged, feeling nobleness inch back up her priority list. "Well, you are the fastest thing I've ever come up against."

"Yeah, I started coming on to you on a snow-packed roof in the middle of a heist. Believe me, babe, not even I have ever moved that fast. I think I set some kind of record."

"You sure did."

"So? Why the kiss-off?"

Nobleness topped the chart, and Chantal let out a heavy sigh. "Maybe we'd better get in, Jaz. It's a long story."

Something in her tone set off a warning bell. "Am I going to regret I asked?"

She was already feeling him slip away, and as much as she wanted to soothe his fears, kiss him one more time, she knew it wouldn't be right. So she offered the only permissible consolation. "I hope not, Jaz."

When they were both inside Jaz reached for the key, and as she had done so many nights before, she stopped him with her hand on his. "We'c better talk first. You just might want to drop me off at my car when we're through."

"Highly unlikely, babe. Unless"—his voice trailec off—"you did something really awful."

Oh, God. Apprehension welled in her breast, and her next words were barely a whisper. "Like what?"

"Like went off and married old what's-his-name." He sighed, dropping his head on the steering wheel. "Don't tell me that, Chantal. Tell me anything else, but don't tell me that."

Under other circumstances, pure relief would have made her laugh, but the truth wasn't much better than his off-the-mark conjecture. "No, Jaz. I didn't marry Roger."

His face remained doubtful. "Anybody else?" What did he know about her social life? He'd monopolized it for forty-eight hours and then she'd kicked him out.

His obvious jealousy buoyed her spirits a bit, and she managed a hesitant smile. "For years there was no one until you, and there's certainly been no one since."

He raised his hand to her face and caressed her cheek with his thumb, his tension easing off. "Then we can handle anything else." He shoved in the clutch and reached for the key, and this time she didn't stop him.

When they were on the highway, headed out of town, he glanced at her. "Okay, babe. I'm listening."

Maybe this was the best way, she thought, in the darkened cab of the Jeep, where she didn't have to look into his eyes. Slowly and softly she began, right from the beginning, leaving nothing out. She told him the truth about her father, her grandfather, and her great-grandfather, all the way down the line. She told him the truth about

Paul and the rainy night on the roof of the Dubois villa. And she told him about her shame and guilt for abandoning her brother.

It was all too familiar for Jaz, and his own guilt increased with every word. Somehow, in his emotional turmoil, he'd neatly forgotten about his duplicity in going behind her back. Damn, he thought. It would be a helluva lot easier not to tell her.

But untold truths were as dangerous as lies, and he wasn't in a gambling mood, not with Chantal's love at stake.

Jaz's silence unnerved Chantal. She twisted her hands in a white-knuckled knot in her lap and wished she'd waited until they were home. What was he thinking? Was he shocked? Disgusted? The dark profile of his face gave away nothing, and she was too afraid to ask. She finished the story as he pulled to a stop in her driveway. If possible, the silence deepened.

She took it for about thirty seconds and then opened her door. He was probably waiting for her to get out so he could leave.

"Wait," he said. "I'll come around and get you."

"That's okay. Don't bother. Good-bye." The words tumbled over one another as she made good her escape, sliding out of the Jeep into the snow.

She heard him come after her and hastened her steps. At the door the keys jingled and jangled in her hand. She didn't want to see his face. She didn't want her last memory to be one of condemnation.

She had fast hands, but not fast enough. With one more lock to go, he bounded up the porch stairs and swung her up into his arms. "Now I'm going to have to buy you a new pair of shoes," he drawled.

"Jaz, put me down. I understand."

"No, Chantal. You don't understand, but you will in a few minutes. Open the door, please."

Why did he have to make this so hard? "Just leave, Jaz. I don't need a lecture." She struggled in his arms, but for every ounce of energy she expended he countered with two, making it clear how thoroughly trapped she was.

"This is a losing game, babe. The door, please." When she reluctantly complied he added, "A lecture isn't what I have in mind. Confession is more like it." Without setting her down, he kicked the door shut behind them. "For starters, for enders, for all the middles, I love you. Nothing is going to change that. Ever."

"Jaz—"

"Don't stop me now. This isn't easy." He paused and inhaled deeply. "I knew about Monte Carlo before I came back from Denver two months ago. At least, I was able to confirm the Dubois scandal and the family business. I pieced together the rest."

Shock stopped her struggles more effectively than his strength. "How?"

"General Moore."

"Why?"

"Because I fell in love in your bathtub. I didn't know it at the time, but when I got on that plane I knew it had to be love. Nothing else hurts in quite the same way."

"Oh, Jaz," she breathed softly. "We've wasted so much time."

"You're not mad?"

"I'm not exactly in a position to be slinging mud."

"Then we're even?" he asked hopefully.

"Oh, yes, Jaz. After all the craziness and danger, after all the secrets, I think we've hit solid ground."

"How about if we hit the bed instead?" He flashed her a wicked grin. "Or am I moving too fast again?"

She smiled sweetly and slid her hand across the front of his shirt, tracing the curves of muscle with her fingertips, remembering and loving the hard warmth of his body. "I think I can keep up with you this time, babe," she murmured close to his ear, then began a slow rediscovery with her tongue. His tie loosened in her fingers and the buttons on his shirt came undone one by one.

"Ummm." He muffled a groan of pleasure along the tender skin of her neck as he carried her to the bed. "It's been too long, Chantal." He lowered her to the floor, his hands sliding up her thighs and pushing her dress higher and higher. "Is there a zipper?"

"Try the bow."

Capturing her mouth with his in a searing kiss, he tugged at the material and felt her unwrap in his arms. "My kind of dress," he whispered against her lips.

She undid his belt and the button fly on his pants. No trace of shyness stayed her hands. She wanted him, not the memories of her dreams.

When their clothes were a pile of blue shimmer and black wool, he sat on the edge of the bed and pulled her into his lap with her legs wrapped around his waist.

"It's been too long," he said against her breasts, teasing and plundering the gentle swells with his tongue and mouth. "Too long without a taste of you, without your touch. Lord, you're sweet. . . . Touch me, Chantal."

And she did, with all the love in her heart, in all the ways he'd taught her in one night.

"I'm hungry."

"You're always hungry." She rolled onto her side and graced him with a purely languorous smile. "How did your poppa ever afford to feed you?"

"Dad's in banking. I think he floated a few loans during my growth years. Do you still have that bottle of ketchup and those crackers?"

She giggled and pressed him back into the pillows. "You must be desperate."

"No, babe, you wore the desperation out of me—"

"Jaz!"

"—and I loved every minute of it, but you left a big hunger." He lifted his head and smacked a kiss on the tip of her nose.

"How does lasagna and chocolate cake sound?"

"Too good to be true. I wish you hadn't mentioned it."

He was beautiful, his rich brown hair fanning out on the pillow, tousled with their lovemaking, his body a sensual pattern of corded muscle and dark skin. Silky strands of gold tumbled over her shoulders and lay in half circles on his chest.

She traced the prominent vein running up his arm and over his biceps. "Do you remember how to work the microwave?"

"I remembered everything else, didn't I?" he asked teasingly, rubbing his hands up and down her satiny skin and lingering around her small waist.

"Then check the refrigerator, Jaz. You're in for a big surprise."

Jaz fed her the last bite of chocolate cake and set the platter on the nightstand. Stretching his arms above his head, he eased back on the pillows, grinning from ear to ear.

"You ate half of a chocolate cake!" she exclaimed. She still couldn't believe it.

"You had three bites," he countered in self-defense, then polished off his third glass of milk.

"And two helpings of lasagna!"

"It was great, babe. I didn't know you had culinary talents."

Chantal cast her eyes heavenward. "I've only got one pound of bacon and a dozen eggs for breakfast. What are we going to do?"

He pulled her into his lap. "I've got a plan," he said, settling her between his spread legs.

She glanced up at him from under a veil of midnight-black lashes. "Sounds dangerous."

"I think we've proved we can handle danger," he drawled lazily, playing his fingers through the blond waves framing her face.

"What's the plan, Jaz?"

"Promise not to panic?"

"I promise," she said solemnly, crossing her finger over her heart, and then she smiled and gave him a little punch. "You know I never panic! I may run like hell, but I never panic!"

The snappy comeback she'd expected never came. A heartbeat passed, and then another, as he gazed searchingly at her. "Marry me, Chantal," he said softly.

Surprise widened her eyes and parted her mouth, but the answer was less than a second from her lips, propelled by the surge of happiness threatening to overwhelm her. "Yes," she gasped out.

"Honeymoon on my private beach in Mexico?"

"Yes," she said with more force.

"No bikini?"

"Yes, yes, yes." Tiny kisses covered his face.

Grinning, he shifted her weight and bent a knee around her hips. "I think I'm on a roll here, babe. Is there anything else I should get while the getting is good?"

She snuggled up closer, pressing a kiss on the

smile crease in his lean cheek. "What else do you want?"

"Another one of those kisses, except a little lower and to the left."

"Don't you think we should wait for the honeymoon?" she said teasingly, not stopping her kisses for a second.

"Practice makes perfect, babe. I figure it will take a week to get our blood tests and license. That's not much time to fine-tune a plan and get all the bugs out." He angled his mouth over hers and said huskily, "We'd better keep at it."

Chantal paced the porch of the beach bungalow with awkward steps, sucking on a wedge of pineapple and holding her fuchsia-pink sarong away from her hips. Every now and then she leveled a baleful glare at her husband.

"Jasper, I swear. If you come up with any more plans, do me a favor and make them solo attempts. "She'd taken to calling him Jasper whenever she was upset. Somehow "Jaz" never had the right bite to it.

"Sorry, babe. I thought an eight sunscreen would do the trick." He was sitting and swinging comfortably in the hammock hanging diagonally across one corner of the porch.

"You can just forget tricks!" she said huffily. His smile lacked the correct amount of contrition for her wounded ego and scorched backside.

He groaned, his grin finally slipping. "Don't remind me. Sweet lady, I'm suffering right along with you. Next time we honeymoon, let's stay home and ski for a week."

"Oh, Jaz." She sighed. "I wanted so much for this week to be perfect. Now I'm a mess."

"You're the prettiest mess I've ever seen." Another grin twitched the corner of his mouth and put a devilish twinkle in his eyes. "That shade of pink is real interesting with that shade of lobster red."

"Don't tease me," she wailed, coming to a halt in front of him.

"I can't help it. You're so teasable and I can't kiss you."

A thoughtful gleam lit the sapphire of her eyes. She pursed her mouth into a pout. "You could if you were real careful."

"Trust me?"

"With my life." She leaned forward as best she could and presented her slightly crisped face.

"Umm, pineapple." He ran his tongue over her lips. "I like it, but you're wearing a strange perfume. What is it?"

She giggled. "Eau de Solarcaine, about fifty cents an ounce. I wonder if things would have turned out differently if I'd been wearing it instead of my French perfume that night on the roof."

"No way, babe." He kissed her once, very carefully, holding his natural instincts in check. He was so used to reaching for her, touching her whenever she was close. "You belong to me. You've always belonged to me, and somehow I sensed it the first time I saw you, not even knowing how beautiful you were or how sweet your voice was."

Chantal edged in closer and rubbed her hands over his shoulders, her pain lessening from his love. "And do you belong to me, Jaz?"

"I always have, babe, since long before I met you." He traced another gentle line across her lips. "I always will."

THE EDITOR'S CORNER

One of the best "presents" I've received at Bantam is the help of the very talented and wonderfully enthusiastic Barbara Alpert, who has written the copy for the back cover of almost every LOVESWEPT romance since the first book. (In fact, only three in all this time haven't been written by Barbara, and I wrote those.) As usual, Barbara has done a superb job of showcasing all the books next month, and so I thought I would give you a sneak peek at her copy on the marvelous books you can expect to keep your holiday spirits high.

First, we are delighted to welcome a brand-new writer—and our first Canadian author—Judy Gill, with **HEAD OVER HEELS**, LOVESWEPT #228. "The sultry laughter and tantalizing aromas that wafted across the fence from next door were enough to make a grown man cry, Buck Halloran thought—or else climb eight-foot fences! But the renowned mountain climber was confined to a wheelchair, casts on one arm and one leg . . . how could he meet the woman behind the smoky voice, the temptress who was keeper of the goodies? . . . He had to touch her, searing her lips with kisses that seduced her heart and soul—and Darcy Gallagher surrendered to the potent magic of his embrace. But the handsome wanderer who whispered sexy promises to her across the hedge at midnight had his eyes on a higher mountain, a new adventure, while she yearned to make a home for children and the man she loved. Could they join their lives and somehow share the dreams that gave them joy?"

Sandra Brown has given us a memorable gift of love in **TIDINGS OF GREAT JOY**, LOVESWEPT #229. As Barbara describes it, "Ria Lavender hadn't planned on spending a passionate Christmas night in front of a roaring fire with Taylor Mackensie. But somehow the scents of pine tree, wood smoke, and male flesh produced a kind of spontaneous combustion inside her, and morning found the lovely architect lying on her silver fox coat beside the mayor-elect, a man she hardly knew. Ten weeks later she knew she was pregnant with Taylor's child . . . and insisted they had to marry. A marriage 'in name only,' she promised him. Taylor agreed to a wedding, but shocked Ria with his demand that they live together as husband and wife—in every way. She couldn't deny she wanted him, the lady-killer with the devil's grin, but

(continued)

there was danger in succumbing to the heat he roused—in falling for a man she couldn't keep."

Prepare yourself for a session of hearty laughter and richly warming emotion when you read Joan Elliott Pickart's **ILLUSIONS,** LOVESWEPT #230. Barbara teases you unmercifully with her summary of this one! "There was definitely a naked man asleep in Cassidy Cole's bathtub! With his ruggedly handsome face and 'kissin' lips,' Sagan Jones was a single woman's dream, and how could she resist a smooth-talking vagabond with roving hands who promised he'd stay only until his luggage caught up with him? Sagan had come to Cherokee, Arizona, after promising Cassidy's brother he'd check up on her. He'd flexed his muscles, smiled his heart-stopping smile, and won over everyone in town except her. . . . Sagan had spent years running from loneliness, and though his lips vowed endless pleasures, Cassidy knew he wasn't a man to put down roots. . . . Could she make him see that in a world full of mirages and dreams that died with day, her love was real and everlasting?"

Hagen strikes again in Kay Hooper's delightful **THE FALL OF LUCAS KENDRICK,** LOVESWEPT #231. As Barbara tells you, "Time was supposed to obscure memories, but when Kyle Griffon saw the sunlight glinting off Lucas Kendrick's hair, she knew she'd never stopped waiting for him. Ten years before, he'd awakened her woman's passion, and when he left without a word, her quicksilver laughter had turned to anger, and her rebel's heart to a wild flirtation with danger—anything to forget the pain of losing him. Now he was back, and he needed her help in a desperate plan— but did she dare revive the flame of desire that once had burned her?" Only Josh, Raven, Rafferty, a few other fictional characters, Kay, Barbara, and I know right now. Be sure that you're one of the first next month to get the answer!

You can have the wish you wish as you read this: another great love story from Iris Johansen who gives you **STAR LIGHT, STAR BRIGHT,** LOVESWEPT #232. "When the golden-haired rogue in the black leather jacket dodged a barrage of bullets to rescue her, Quenby Swenson thrilled . . . with fear and with excitement," says Barbara most accurately. "Gunner Nilsen had risked his life to save her, but when he promised to cherish her for a lifetime, she refused to believe him. And yet she knew somehow he'd

(continued)

never lie to her, never hurt her, never leave her—even though she hardly knew him at all. He shattered her serenity, rippled her waters, vowing to play her body like the strings of a harp . . . until he'd learned all the melodies inside her. Quenby felt her heart swell with yearning for the dreams Gunner wove with words and caresses. Did she dare surrender to this mysterious man of danger, the untamed lover who promised her their souls were entwined for all time?"

For one of the most original, whimsical, and moving romances ever, you can't beat **THE BARON,** LOVESWEPT #233 by Sally Goldenbaum. Barbara whets your appetite with this terrific description: "Disguised as a glittering contessa for a glamorous mystery weekend, Hallie Finnegan knew anything was possible—even being swept into the arms of a dashing baron! She'd never been intriguing before, never enchanted a worldly man who stunned her senses with hungry kisses beneath a full moon. Once the 'let's pretend mystery' was solved, though, they shed their costumes, revealing Hallie for the shy librarian with freckles she was— but wealthy, elegant Nick Harrington was still the baron . . . and not in her league. When Nick turned up on her doorstep in pursuit of his fantasy lady, Hallie was sure he'd discover his mistake and run for the hills!"

It's a joy for me to send you the same heartfelt wishes for the season that we've sent you every year since LOVE-SWEPT began. May your New Year be filled with all the best things in life—the company of good friends and family, peace and prosperity, and of course, love.

Warm wishes for 1988 from all of us at LOVESWEPT.

Sincerely,

Carolyn Nichols

Carolyn Nichols
  Editor
LOVESWEPT
Bantam Books, Inc.
666 Fifth Avenue
New York, NY 10103